SERENITY *Dance*

wishing you
abundant blessings, peace,
joy, and continued success!
Danielle Wainwright

Danielle Wainwright

Dog Ear Publishing
INDIANAPOLIS, IN

Dog Ear Publishing
4011 Vincennes Rd.
Indianapolis, IN 46268
www.dogearpublishing.net

Copyediting and Design by Hallagen Ink (www.HallagenInk.com)

Serenity Dance: The First Steps / Danielle Wainwright.—1st ed.

ISBN 978-145752-945-0

To my mother Inosia.

To my beautiful daughters Alexandra and Angeline.

To Haiti.

To God be the glory!

God grant me the serenity
To accept the things I cannot change;
Courage to change the things I can;
And wisdom to know the difference...

—REINHOLD NIEBUHR

Chapter One

GABRIELLE IFEYA NAMID'S flight to Germany was scheduled for just after eleven o'clock in the morning on her seventeenth birthday. Outside, the shimmering, wavy lines generated from the radiating heat spread wildly across the tarmac as the planes taxied to their designated spots around the Port–au-Prince airport.

As Gabrielle approached the entrance, she lifted her arm in an attempt to wipe away a band of sweat that began to form across her forehead. Benji kept a pace of two steps ahead of her, carrying her heavy suitcase in one arm and keeping one hand free in case she needed assistance. Gabrielle looked ahead at him, marveling at how his white linen shirt and khaki pants had managed to stay dry despite the heat. She was grateful that he had taken a break from his hectic class schedule at Faculté des Sciences to take her to the airport so they could say goodbye at the gate, her last footsteps in Haiti.

"Almost there, love," Benji said, glancing over his shoulder. She smiled up at him, taking in how the sunlight bounced off his facial features. At twenty-one years old, Benji's features had grown nicely into strong cheekbones and jawline, contrasting his soft brown eyes.

Despite the weight of the bags in tote, Gabrielle managed to adeptly distribute her weight and walk gracefully through the airport's front doors in her black four-inch-high heels. She gripped tightly to her purse that cleverly matched her sundress and the tote bag Elodie, her mother, had given her for her birthday. The tote, large enough to hold the entire contents of her nightstand, held her precious journals, of which she packed four blank ones in case she had difficulty finding them in Germany. In addition were some colored pencils for doodling and a pouch holding personal contents, such as any jewelry she wasn't already wearing.

Benji arrived at the counter first and turned to take hold of Gabrielle's other bags while she fished through her handbag to find her papers. After retrieving them, she handed over her flight ticket, passport, and green card. The attendant looked at the papers and then up at Gabrielle. "Joli prénom," she said.

In recent years, Gabrielle had grown accustomed to accepting compliments on her name, but even more so, for her stunning features. She somehow managed to bypass the awkward teen years and quickly developed right into a creature of beauty. Several inches taller than her friends, and even most of her family, she learned quickly to carry her five-foot-ten stature with graceful confidence. The rest—her radiant complexion, the sparkle in her eyes, and the small dimples that punctuated her mouth like a semi-colon—all followed suit, making her nothing short of striking. Together, she and Benji turned heads everywhere they went.

The agent returned her paperwork, including the boarding pass and freshly stamped passport that was now dated July 1, 1979. Gabrielle turned to face Benji. She knew intuitively that her smile couldn't camouflage the sadness in her heart. Not to him. He knew better than anyone that there was sadness behind her upturned lips. They had avoided talking too much about the day she would leave. Instead, they filled their days with long walks and going to the movies. She had shared with him her plans about how the days would be after she left. The ones that kept her excited for her future life in Germany that Edgar, her half-brother, and Essie, her sister-in-law, had guaranteed her. But, there was little mention of the sorrowful goodbye that she and Benji would have to endure.

What kept Gabrielle focused on her plans was hearing about the American army base and the apartment nearby that Edgar and his family lived in. Edgar granted her the promise of an enriching life away from the poverty-stricken streets of Haiti and the political discourse that made some people want to flee, as she was, to anywhere but there. It had been a month since Edgar sent for Gabrielle, and now that the first of July was here, she fought with the dichotomy of exhilaration and emotional exhaustion. When Gabrielle talked about what was to come for her in Germany, she made it sound rather glamorous both in her voice and her hand gestures. Benji would listen, nod, and hold tight to her hand. The one thing they both knew was that he held Haiti in high regard. He would graduate from Faculté des Sciences at the same time Gabrielle would finish high school in Germany. With his degree in civil engineering, Benji dreamed of making a difference on the same streets that so many of his fellow citizens chose to flee.

"Everyone here faces unemployment rates that are extraordinary and daunting," he had told Gabrielle in one of their recent conversations. "But, that doesn't deter me from wanting to be a part of the transformation."

She understood, and even more so, she admired his commitment to his country.

Gabrielle gathered her carry-on belongings again, looking past the agent to watch as her luggage was swept away by the conveyor belt. Benji took hold of Gabrielle's free hand as they made their way toward the departure gate. Each person Gabrielle passed as she weaved through the crowd was filled with heightened emotions. Airports had a way of doing that, and it only added to Gabrielle's combating feelings of anxiety and excitement. She felt that most of those she passed by were either leaving the country or hoping for their own way to escape to a better life. She sensed all their emotions, ranging from hope and anticipation to sadness and sorrow. Some stood open-armed and smiling as they greeted travelers returning home. Others tightly embraced departing loved ones, wishing to be boarding the same departing plane instead of having to walk back out of the airport, into the heat, and their familiar lives. The moment of dropping someone off at the airport meant a small taste of escape and faraway places.

"Are you nervous about the flight?" Benji asked, breaking the thick air of silence.

She felt his grip on her hand tighten slightly.

"No, not too nervous. Edgar assured me it is an easy flight. He and Essie had no problems with theirs, and I expect the same." She tightened her own grip by wrapping all five fingers around his hand. Her sinewy hands with freshly painted nails, a treat from Essie who had sent her nail polish for her birthday, meant even her hands were stunning.

What Gabrielle did not share with Benji was that her bed sheets had been left tied in a large knot from tossing and turning all night. She had woken up several times, and at one point turned on the light so she could try to capture her thoughts in her journal. The ongoing battle through the night left her frustrated enough that for the first time since she started keeping a journal, she was unable to find the words to adequately express her emotions. By dawn, she had resorted to only doodling on a few pages. With just a few hours of sleep, Gabrielle was up and about by six o'clock, packing her essential belongings and taking care of last minute tasks. Her mother had promised to take care of washing her bed sheets, and addressing anything else that was left behind, knowing Gabrielle was not planning to return for a very long time, if ever.

As they approached the gate, Gabrielle looked with curiosity at the plane outside the oversized window. It was taxied and about ready to board, according to the announcement on the loud speaker. The flight information for her initial flight to Miami was displayed over the gate's door and several people gathered around. She imagined the flight crew was prepping the interior so they could board.

Benji let go of her hand and placed both of his own on her shoulders. Turning her toward him he said, "je t'aime, Gaby." The tears welled up in his eyes, not quite ready to be released. He wasn't one to readily show his feelings, but there had always been something about Gabrielle that made him react differently. He softened in her presence and she made him feel things he hadn't felt before. Most knew him as the engineer he was—analytical, self-sufficient, and stoic. Gabrielle melted away those characteristics in ways no one else had before.

"I love you, too." Gabrielle leaned in and whispered in his ear, brushing his cheek with her lips. Laughing only for a moment, she reached up and wiped the imprint of red lipstick from his cheek. "I promise to write every day," she said.

Benji nodded, but said nothing, and wrapped his arms around her. She could feel his thoughts in the pounding of his heart against her chest.

The stewardess broke their moment when she announced the boarding of her flight. Gabrielle unlocked her eyes from Benji and noticed that one by one, everyone was starting to board their flight. She became one of a few who waited until the moment of last boarding call. It was then when she finally stepped back from Benji and looked one last time into his warm, brown eyes. Too choked up to speak, they kissed once more before she turned touched his nose with her fingertip, forced a smile, and walked to the gate. Just before the plank, she turned and ran back to him.

"Someday we will be together again. I love you," she said. Before he could respond, Gabrielle turned and ran down the plank to board the plane, allowing one welled up tear to set free and roll down her cheek. Benji exited the airport before his own warm tears finally released and rolled down his cheeks.

In her window seat, Gabrielle looked outside at the parking lot where she was certain she saw Benji walking. His back was to her, and the parking lot far away, but she would know him anywhere. Finally, the rest of her tears fell.

Gabrielle gripped her tote bag and thought about the craziness that her entire life was packed up and on the plane about to head to a foreign land; no belongings, however, could match the love she felt for Benji, and the struggle she endured in leaving him behind. It was that struggle that she had wrestled with all night, but by dawn, she also knew she was making the right move and that from that day forward, her life would never be the same.

I

THE LANDING IN Miami was bumpy due to a crop of thunderstorms in the area. Once its wheels hit the ground, the plane taxied across the tarmac to its gate. Eventually the stewardess swung the door open, allowing in a small breeze of humid Florida air. Exiting the plane was slow moving while passengers made their way down the aisle and out the small door that led them to the walkway and eventually the terminal.

Once inside the airport, Gabrielle's assigned immigration guard struggled to keep pace with her long-legged stride. With too much time on her hands until her next flight, she wasn't sure how she was going to cope, let alone in the company of a stranger whose sole purpose that day was to accompany her every move. Despite her legal green card, and a final destination of Germany, the immigration guard was sent to ensure she didn't try to sneak out of the airport in order to stay in the United States.

Gabrielle found a bench near the gate to sit on. She peeled off pieces of a croissant and occasionally sipped from a cup of hot coffee that she set on the table next to her.

"It's not like I need you to shadow me," she said as she glanced up at the guard. He had sat down across from her and two seats down. "Look at my ticket if you want. It isn't like I want to stay anywhere near here. I am heading to Germany where I will live with my brother. I have no interest in a life in Florida...here in your United States." What Gabrielle didn't tell him was that she did indeed plan on returning to Florida for college. She had begun researching schools near Miami, but hadn't settled on one. With the busy year of school ahead of her, she would tackle the rest of that task in the spring. But, for now, Germany was her destination.

Her words fell on the immigration agent's deaf ears. His response was to ignore her and shake his newspaper out, reading and turning pages. He did, however, keep a close watch on Gabrielle with one eye and the paper with the other. She noticed how his wide fingers gripped the newspaper and wondered if he was even reading the pages. After a few minutes of the guard paying her no mind, she shifted her thoughts to holding hands with Benji. His were always warm and soft to the touch. He sometimes wrapped just a few fingers around her wrist and gently guided her as they walked through town to the cinema. She never knew why he liked holding onto her wrist. It wasn't that he didn't hold her hand, he certainly did. That was more often saved for inside the cinema or when just the two of them walked alone down a side street. Holding her wrist was one of his quirky ways of showing affection that made him even more endearing to her.

The light thrown from the movie screen was always just enough for them to be able to see one another, but not so much that other cinema goers could spot them kissing. Not the details anyway. Everyone's shadows bounced off the walls, especially during the brighter scenes. However, most kisses were stolen in the back row with no one behind them, and most especially when the light was dim. That didn't mean that giggles could not be heard throughout the rows as girls felt their knees being touched or a hand tickling the back of their neck. The fun and innocence that ensued in each couple's seat kept the regulars going back each week. It was one of the many pastimes Gabrielle knew she would miss about Haiti and sharing with her Benji.

IN THE AIRPORT, a family of seven made its way past Gabrielle, with the two smallest children hanging onto their mother's arms. They were screaming and the mother looked exhausted. Gabrielle thought she recognized them from the Port-au-Prince airport earlier that day, but she couldn't be certain. There had been many families waiting to board different flights or waiting for loved ones to arrive at their gates. Gabrielle watched as the father scooped up one of the crying children and put her up on his shoulders. The other three children carried bags nearly bigger than themselves and stared doe-eyed ahead. Gabrielle hoped for their sake that their gate wasn't too far away. She imagined they weren't going to Germany, and that their final destination would be where they hoped to start a new life, free of the Haitian politics, famine, and depression.

Seeing the family tugged at Gabrielle's heart. She thought of her mother, home in bed with a hot cup of tea. Elodie hadn't been feeling well the past few days and Gabrielle insisted she stay home instead of coming to the airport where she would only further jeopardize her immune system. Earlier that morning they had said their goodbyes and gave kisses on each other's cheeks. Benji waited outside with her suitcases. He knew Gabrielle and Elodie needed privacy to say their goodbyes, and he didn't want to intrude. He also knew that Gabrielle's mother wasn't privy to very much about their relationship, and that Elodie would have made assumptions that were unwarranted. For these reasons, Benji learned a while ago to stay out of their way.

Gabrielle had left her mother's room that morning, knowing that Elodie was angry and hurt because Gabrielle was leaving with no intended date of return. As Gabrielle finally made her way through the door and outside to the fresh air and Benji waiting for her, she felt a shift within her that was unfamiliar, yet liberating.

I

AFTER THE LAST bite of her croissant, Gabrielle stood to throw out the tissue it had been wrapped in. "Don't worry. I'm only walking over to the garbage can," she said to the immigration guard who looked like he was about to stand up to follow her. Gabrielle had seen the glance from the corner of his eye as she stood, and knew he'd either follow her or at least question where she was going. Part of her wanted to go somewhere just so he would have to get up, but a bigger part of her didn't want to pick up her carry-on bags and lug them out of vengeance. Instead, she tossed the tissue in the receptacle across the way. When she turned around to go back to her seat, another family, this time of six, was making its way down the hallway. She waited to let them pass through with their luggage. She had no idea that international traveling would mean a seemingly intentional focus on families. Back in Haiti, she hadn't paid too much attention to families. They were everywhere, of course, but there was something about the airport that was triggering her in a different way. Seeing the parents and their children in motion with a desired goal to travel and change their lives, their camaraderie, stirred the desire deep within to someday have a family of her own. Gabrielle thought about Benji and how they could have given that to one another, but only if she had stayed. She had chosen a different path for the time being, one that he couldn't have walked with her.

"Have you even considered staying?" He once asked. He had asked, but after a noncommittal response, he gave up, as part of her hoped he would. There was, however, another part of her that had hoped he'd fight for her to stay. She struggled with how readily he dropped the subject, and saw it as him letting her go. She wished he had fought harder, but also knew that she needed to do this for herself.

Benji was four years older than her. In his early twenties, he was ready to graduate college and begin his career. She was still a high school girl who had growing up to do before they could be together. So, when Edgar first started inviting her to Germany, Gabrielle saw the move as her chance to almost catch up to

Benji, to become a woman he would want to be with rather than a girl he was dating. She would almost joke about it with Benji, but he would just smile and hold her hand tightly or kiss her on the cheek, as though he had no idea what to say and his affectionate gestures would speak for him. But, to Gabrielle, it only made it seem like the subject of her staying was being dismissed, and her resolve to leave was affirmed.

"YOUR FLIGHT LEAVES in less than an hour. They should be boarding in a bit," said the immigration guard. Gabrielle looked over at him. Lost in her thoughts, she had almost forgotten he was there, almost. With the abrupt reminder, she sat back down and fished through her tote bag for her boarding pass. This time there would be no waiting for the last boarding call. She would board as soon as she could to escape her guard, settle into her seat, and begin the next phase of the journey. For the next twenty minutes until they started boarding, Gabrielle clenched her boarding pass and bags as though she was at the front line of a running race waiting for the gun to pop. Finally, the speaker above squawked and she bid a brief farewell to her immigration guard and handed her boarding pass to the stewardess. No glance back, just two feet forward and into the plane that would take her transatlantic to Mannheim, Germany.

Chapter Two

GABRIELLE'S TEARS SLOWED by the time the pilot announced the seat belt sign had been turned off and passengers were free to move about the cabin. She smiled in an attempt to hide behind her tear-stained cheeks as she looked at the old woman next to her.

"Excuse me," Gabrielle said as she started to slide out of her seat. The woman stood and let her by, smiling in return, but saying nothing.

Making her way down the aisle, Gabrielle held onto the backs of seats for support as she walked. Some of the passengers looked up as she passed while others were buried in newspapers, books, or slumber. Gabrielle thought about how awful she must have looked, but once she was in the closet-sized commode, she saw the damage wasn't as bad as she had anticipated. Finally able to splash cold water on her face, she whispered to the mirror, "Why is it splashing water on your face always makes things better?"

She reached for a paper towel to blot her face dry, and as she looked once again in the mirror, she reminded herself that she would have the gift of a full life ahead of her. Benji would never leave Haiti; she knew that. It saddened her that he didn't have the same excitement about life and its unlimited possibilities that she had. Yet, at the same time she respected his commitment to his homeland and his career. She wondered where he was and what he might be doing—whether he was at the cinema watching a show on the big screen just so he could sit and think about how they shared candy and kisses in the dark. Or whether he was walking down their favorite paths that lead them away from the crowded streets to their special tree. The one where she would lean her back against it and he would lean in to kiss her until she pulled away, always giggling. Most likely, she gathered, he was at home studying. Like her, he had always been a one of the best students in his classes. He would graduate with honors, ensuring him of an engineering career. He was on his right path.

The second splash of cold water was more practical than anything. She added a dab of moisturizer to her cheeks. The salt of the tears had dried her skin, and the added moisture of the tap water helped the lotion absorb into her skin. She felt refreshed for the first time in several hours and stole one more glance in the mirror and a look at her long, fine, dark hair that flowed down her back the way her mother's did. Elodie used to fix it for her every morning before school, tugging out the knots with a brush. Gabrielle cried when she tugged too hard. But, when she thought of how horrid short hair would look, which was what Elodie threatened if Gabrielle fussed, she endured the brush strokes, wincing through each one. It wasn't until she was old enough to fix it on her own when she realized that indeed, it was hard to not tug, and she slowly forgave her mother.

Even still, Gabrielle never really liked the way Elodie styled her hair once the knots were eventually out. Gabrielle would wait until she left home to fix it how she liked it, and in the afternoon she would put it back the way Elodie had set it that morning. She couldn't wait until the day she was old enough to style her own hair without resistance from her mother. When that day came, the friction of the morning battles diminished.

GABRIELLE KNEW THE news of moving to Germany to live with Edgar broke Elodie's heart. Edgar was much older than Gabrielle, and Elodie suspected he wanted to give her the chance at a different life. In order to expedite her move, and to give Gabrielle their father's name, Edgar went through the motions to legally adopt her. She had been given Elodie's last name at birth, but for the first time in her seventeen years, she felt a semblance of a connection to her father's side of the family.

"Elodie, the name change goes with the adoption. It will allow the transition to go smoother. It's not against you in anyway," he had explained. Gabrielle was sitting on the couch that day, listening as Edgar laid out the details of her upcoming move to Germany.

"I understand," was all Elodie could say. She had no logical reason to fight the adoption or the move. Edgar's promises were compelling.

"She'll attend her last year of high school at the Mannheim American High School with other kids on base. It's a chance of a lifetime. I want to give her this." After those words, Edgar had stood and said goodbye. "I have a few more things to take care of before I leave to head back to Germany," he said to Elodie, then turned to Gabrielle. "I'll see you in Germany. Emmanuel and Essie will be glad to have you. I think you'll like the change of scenery, and of course, the school."

"Thank you, Edgar." Gabrielle stood from the couch and walked him to the door.

"Are you sure you are okay with all of this?" Gabrielle asked Elodie after Edgar left.

"It's a chance you'll never have again. You should go and not worry about me," said Elodie.

The adoption was final before Edgar left Haiti to return to Germany. Even though Elodie respected the decision and did her best not to get in the way, her emotions were another matter. On the one hand, she had come this far raising her daughter, and felt as though she had given her opportunities with schooling that most girls her age did not have. On the other hand, she knew that Edgar could give Gabrielle a life beyond the boundaries of Haiti, as well as serve as a father figure. It was Elodie's acceptance of those two elements that allowed her to relinquish, reluctant as she was.

Many Haitians had traveled to the United States, where the mystery of the land of opportunity was unveiled to them. Some returned, unimpressed by their experiences, but others relished in their new homes.

New York City was often seen as a foreign country, not just a city. In contrast to Haitian weather, New York City was perceived as cold, snowy, and crowded. This belief permeated various aspects of the Haitian psyche. It even found its way into the repertoire of a Haitian musical group. The group recorded a song about the difficulties around Haitians getting up in the morning to catch a bus to work or school in New York. And yet, the people back home thought they were living it up in the Big Apple. Things couldn't be so bad because they were in the land of opportunity. To most Haitians, any other country was better than home. But their perception wasn't reality. The musical group tried to show the dichotomy of the illusion versus the reality, but it never really changed people's view.

For a while, Miami, on the other hand, was merely the gateway to New York City, or just another city. A passport and a ticket to Miami still meant a promising future. It was as though the symbolism of the stamp on the passport was equivalent to promising days ahead. Because of this, travel had become a status symbol for those who had the resources to travel outside the country, often for vacation or to seek medical attention. The juxtaposition of the rich and the poor was startling. At the same time, many were content with the known and left the unknown to the adventurists.

Having witnessed these dynamics over her young years, and ever since she was a child, Gabrielle had watched the planes fly overhead and knew that one day she would be on one. She didn't know until recently where that plane would take her, but she knew the oblong vehicle with wings would be her salvation.

"Germany is far away, Gaby," Elodie had said when the plans first came up. "You're sure?"

They were in the kitchen cooking dinner one night when Gabrielle had read out loud to her mother a letter from Edgar. The letter preceded Edgar's last visit to Haiti, the one when he officially adopted Gabrielle. However, this particular letter came with the promise of a one-way plane ticket for her and word of his plans to visit Haiti to work out all of the details.

He and Gabrielle had met before, at family functions, and he had immediately taken on a protective parental role with her, extending past his big brother status. Now, when Gabrielle held his letter in her hand, she knew she had to be on the flight he promised. From their prior conversations, Edgar also knew Gabrielle wouldn't refuse it. She had shared with him her passion for school, and her desire to be a teacher or businesswoman.

One particular night at a family party when Gabrielle was about fifteen, she asked him about Germany and what it was like. Her eyes grew wide as he told her of the land that was so foreign to her, and yet so inviting at the same time. She could not have guessed then that he would be able to arrange to not only adopt her, but to bring her to Mannheim. Even still, two years later, and as she read his letter, she was a bit surprised by the level of excitement the idea of moving stirred within her. For many in the Haitian population at the time, a one-way ticket out was likened to winning the lottery, and that was exactly how Edgar had made her feel.

"Mom, I can't explain why; I just know it's what I must do. I have to go." Gabrielle tucked the letter in its envelope. "He's offering me an education that I can't get here. He writes here that I can attend the Mannheim American High School. Where else would I have that chance? I can make something of myself." Gabrielle held up the envelope, but it was only for emphasis. She knew her mother wouldn't take it and read the letter again.

"Stay here, settle down, Gaby. Why must you go far away?" Her mother's words barely made their way off her tongue. It was her last attempt, and a weak one at that, because she knew it was fruitless. She turned toward the sink and put her head in her hands with the dishtowel between them.

"I love the idea of a new life more," Gabrielle's heart sank. She did not relish in hurting her mother, and quietly wished the time would pass quickly between then and when she would leave. "I know I am hurting you, but Edgar is offering me a life I could not possibly make on my own. I'm only seventeen, mother. I have so much to live for. I want to live it, not settle." With that Gabrielle stood from the table. "I'm sorry," she said and left the room.

As she walked down the hall to her bedroom, she whispered to herself, "God grant me the serenity to accept the things I cannot change; courage to change the things I can; and wisdom to know the difference." The Serenity Prayer was her source of relief from emotional turbulence, and in this moment, it was all she had to turn to.

From her bedroom, Gabrielle could hear her mother crying in the kitchen. She felt guilty knowing that Elodie could not understand her desires for more. Sitting on her bed, Gabrielle thought about Edgar's upcoming visit, the flight he promised to book for her, and what life in Germany would be like. Even though it petrified her, the lure was stronger than the fear.

When the time came and Edgar made the arrangements, Gabrielle knew she had to board that flight on the first of July. Just weeks before her flight, she looked around her room, sized up the number of suitcases she would need, and considered what she was willing to leave behind. She was a bit surprised to discover that she really didn't have much that she wanted to take with her. There were only a few sentimental items she would take, but the rest represented her old life and didn't belong in the underbelly of a plane that would take her to Miami and then on to Germany. The decision had been made, and she began packing.

I

GABRIELLE UNLATCHED THE bathroom door just as the plane hit turbulence. High heels were not meant for high altitude bumps. She tactfully made her way back to her seat before the pilot put the fasten seatbelt sign back on and announced that they were going through a storm, but he didn't expect it to last long. After squeezing by the woman next to her, and buckling back in, Gabrielle lay back and looked out the window into the dark clouds until she drifted off.

Some time later Gabrielle was awoken by the sounds of the stewardess, who had made her way down the aisle offering drinks.

"Orange juice, please," a gentleman in a seat near Gabrielle said. She couldn't see him, but could tell by his graveled voice that he was elderly.

While waiting for the stewardess, Gabrielle took out her journal and her favorite pen. When she was at home, in her room, she spent many nights writing poetry. Along with the Serenity Prayer, writing poetry, or even just her thoughts, was her escape. The prayer was for coping with everyday emotional stress, whereas her poetry had everything to do with Benji. By the time she left home, she had written enough poems to fill a book.

Once a week she would submit a poem to the radio station and they would always read it on the air. Each one was dedicated to Benji, who would tune into the radio and listen to the dedication made over the airwaves. Some of their friends were inspired and began writing poetry as well, but none of them ever had the guts to submit them to the radio station. It became Gabrielle and Benji's weekly tribute to their love. She wrote and he listened.

Gabrielle knew that the coming months would be very difficult, and many more poems would be written, filling the pages of her blank journals. Looking out through the plane's window at the black sky, the darkness reflected the emptiness she felt in her heart. The only way she could cope with the heartache in that moment was to write Benji a poem. Though she would probably never send it to him, she would save it for when they next saw each other, and would perhaps send it to the radio station.

If Today

If today I'm living in exile,
Away from your love
It is nature's proof that she is in charge
Living without you by my side
Living without your love
Sweeter than honey
Opened my eyes to how much
You mean to me
Just like the soil needs
Fertilizer to grow
My heart needs you to beat
My heart needs you
To warm my lonely nights
With your tenderness
To keep it alive
I need your water

To quench my thirst for love
I need your hand in mine
To let you know that
I am forever yours
I need to rest my heart against yours
To know that I'm still alive

When Gabrielle finished, she read the poem over again few times. Finally, she put down her pen and tucked the journal back in her bag. Already emotionally drained, she didn't shed any more tears; instead, she let out a sigh. After pushing the tray back up into the back of the seat in front of her, she rested her head against the tiny pillow the stewardess had given her. The woman next to her was breathing heavily as she slept, wearing a mask to cover her eyes, even though the plane was already rather dark. Gabrielle wished in that moment that she, too, had a mask to hide behind. A black satin one would suit her just fine.

WITH GABRIELLE AT just seventeen, and Benji at twenty-one years old, she knew there had been other girlfriends before her, but she also knew that none of them matched the mutual feelings they shared. The simplicity of their love, even the naivety, blessed them in every light kiss and touch between them.

From the day they first met, right up until the moment he put her on the plane in Port-au-Prince, represented a capsule of time that would last a lifetime in their hearts. That was the sentiment she cherished in order to make it through the rough tides. There was solace in the knowing that they shared something so unique. To have something so special at a young age meant she could carry it with her everywhere as she went through life. It showed in her poetry. It showed in the enrichment of the caring she showed others. And, it showed in the love she felt for herself.

Gabrielle and Benji had officially met because of her friendship with his sister, Sasha, who was in the same class as Gabrielle. Sasha had invited Gabrielle home with her to study math, Benji's specialty. He was more than happy to help his sister's new friend solve math equations over the dining room table as they ate afternoon snacks. When he walked in the living room, their eyes met and a silence fell across the room. Moments later it was broken by Sasha urging Gabrielle to pay attention.

Sasha and Gabrielle also shared a love for jewelry; that meant anything from necklaces to bracelets to earrings. When Edgar came to visit Haiti, he brought Gabrielle a jewelry making kit. From that day on, she spent hours threading beads for family, friends, and sometimes for herself. She had the more natural talent and an eye for the craft than Sasha did. Each one of Gabrielle's pieces was unique and made with great care and thoughtfulness. Sasha, on the other hand, tended to string and talk at the same time, which meant detail suffered. Gabrielle listened, but kept a laser eye on the beads and strings. Her results were truly beautiful. Her most special piece was the one Benji wore; a dark brown rope bracelet she had made for him after they first started dating.

When Gabrielle first grew close to Sasha, she let her borrow a gold bracelet that her mother had given her for her fifteenth birthday. Shortly after, Sasha lost the bracelet. Elodie was so upset with Gabrielle that after she duly disciplined her, Elodie took Gabrielle to Sasha's house with her and asked for the bracelet back. Benji was the only one home. He politely told Elodie that parents should not be so overly concerned about the happenings between two friends at school. He explained that the bracelet being lost was an unfortunate incident, but there was little they could do. Benji didn't know that Sasha had revealed to Gabrielle that their father was a jewelry maker. To Benji's surprise, Elodie insisted on a replacement for the bracelet. But Benji held his ground, a quality that struck Gabrielle as masculine and very attractive. She stood in embarrassment on the steps behind her mother, and by the end of the exchange, Gabrielle had wished she was meeting this handsome boy under different circumstances. Defeated, Elodie left and that was the end of the incident. In spite of everything, Gabrielle and Sasha's friendship blossomed, and as such so did her time with Benji. The next time Gabrielle was at their house was when she was studying with Sasha, and she will always remember the look on his face when he walked in the room and saw her again—this time under better pretenses.

As Gabrielle and Benji's relationship grew, there were times when they were given the chance to be alone and could sneak out to the movies. It was in the darkness of the cinema that their love brightened and grew.

IN THE BACK of Gabrielle's mind, she was not quite sure why Benji took her leaving for Germany as well as he did. Never one for drama, she remained ambivalent because she knew he loved her. It was common for those who left Haiti to have their relationship at home fall apart once they got to their foreign country, as they would both eventually find someone new and move on. Gabrielle had seen it happen with some of her friends. It went with the territory of separation and the temptation of new people and experiences.

Even with that, she still had to wonder if she and Benji would be different. Both as a woman and being younger than him, she was the more emotional one. He feigned ambivalence and covered his feelings with understanding by saying he knew it was difficult, but in life they have to do what they must. When they discussed her move, he repeatedly took the cliché and correct way of balancing making her feel good about her decision with not pressing her to change her mind. She didn't know whether to be grateful for it or to be upset that he didn't fight harder for her to stay.

Right up until the last moment, he acted only in kindness and love toward her, and she felt it was because he wanted her to have that image of him to remember him by. There is no worse feeling than an ending to a relationship that leaves stains that don't need to be there.

"We'll stay in touch and we'll see how things go once you get there," he had said. His words left Gabrielle with an underlying fear that the relationship would never be the same. She had believed their love could handle the long distance, at least for a while, until she finished school in Germany. She wanted to be sure to leave that door slightly open. Anything less would have shattered her.

I

WHERE AM I? Gabrielle wondered as she was startled awake by the plane bumping down the runway in Frankfurt. People around her were shifting in their seats, looking out their windows at the gate, and collecting their belongings. When the plane came to a stop and the captain shut off the seat belt sign, everyone stood in near unison to exit. Gabrielle was only twelve rows back, making her exit from the plane relatively fast.

Like Gabrielle, Edgar stood out in a crowd. She spotted his tall physique and dark complexion right away as she made her way through the crowd to greet him. His hug was firm, his voice deep, and as he took her bags he said, "Welcome to Frankfurt!"

Filled with unexpected uncertainty, they approached the baggage claim area. Gabrielle craved seeing that her belongings were intact, and the sense of familiarity.

"Wait here while I grab your luggage," said Edgar.

Gabrielle stood back from the rotating cargo belt, gripping her carry-on bags while he readied himself to grab her luggage from the turnstile.

"It's that one there!" Gabrielle pointed to the approaching, large dark brown bag.

"Got it!" he proclaimed. He easily swept the heavy bag off the conveyor belt and walked over to Gabrielle. "The car is just outside, let's head home."

"Lead the way." Gabrielle struggled to keep pace with him as they exited the airport.

Once outside, Gabrielle noticed and welcomed the cooler air. Used to extreme heat and stifling humidity, she relished in the ability to take a deep breath, fully filling her lungs. As Edgar put her luggage in the back of their station wagon, she climbed in the front passenger seat. The cleanliness of the car made her wonder if their home was equally well kept. She liked a tidy bedroom, and was even in the habit of making her bed every day. Her clothes were always neatly folded in their dresser drawers or hung in order in her closet, but there were certainly times when her jewelry beads were spread out across her bed while she worked on her latest necklace or bracelet. Her journals could also be found spread out on the floor next to her bed after a night of doodling and writing. She realized she wouldn't be able to do that at Edgar's. Her privacy, especially in her journals, was something she had always protected. Edgar's son, Emmanuel, was at an age where he was old enough to be curious—and even to understand—enough of her entries.

"The ride home is about an hour, so settle in and enjoy the views," Edgar said as he sat in the driver's seat and turned the key.

Gabrielle soon discovered just how fast people drive on the autobahn. They were headed to Frankenthal and along the way she couldn't help but notice all of the tall buildings, and how much bigger everything seemed to be compared to Haiti. Even with those observations, she wasn't able to capture the scenery as well as she wanted to since it flew by so fast.

"When does the snowy season start?" she asked, figuring what better icebreaker than talking about snow?

"Not until November or even December. It's surprisingly later in the season than you would think. We have a pretty fall here, so you will have the chance to see the leaves change colors and drop. That seems to be Essie's favorite time of year here. I prefer spring when everything comes back into bloom and the days are longer again." Edgar put on his signal and changed lanes, letting a 1965 Porsche 911 pass them by. "Winter can be long, but it's not too cold. You'll see," he said.

About thirty minutes into the drive, the tall buildings were replaced by residential spreads.

"Oh, and the Mannheim American High School is expecting you this fall. I'm sure I explained to you that it's a school for the military kids. Emmanuel really likes his teachers. He learned to fit in just fine, so I am sure you will figure out everything, too. You will do well enough since you keep good grades."

Gabrielle sat back and absorbed this information. She felt apprehensive about a new school. She didn't feel overly prepared, like she normally would want to be. She also recognized that she had a few months to adjust before the first day of classes, and may even be able to meet a few of the kids ahead of time.

"How's Essie?" she asked, keeping the conversation going.

"She's excited for you to be here. Expect to help her in the kitchen though. The base is where you two will do the shopping. Everything we need is right there. She'll show you. Your room is big enough, I'm sure. Emmanuel knows well enough to leave your things alone, but let me know if there are any issues with him. He needs to hear it from me. He just listens better that way. Essie tries to discipline him, but it's me that he ultimately pays attention to." Edgar looked over at Gabrielle. "She'll tell him to clean his room five times, and I only need to say it once. So, if he gives you any trouble, let me know."

He put his eyes back on the road and Gabrielle nodded her head in affirmation. "I'm sure we'll get along well. Kids like me," she said.

"So did you leave anyone special behind?" Edgar asked, catching Gabrielle off guard with his question.

"Mom wasn't too happy about it, as you might have gathered," she said, not knowing what else to say.

"That I would expect. She'll see soon enough what a good decision you made. But, what about a boyfriend? Break any hearts in Port-au-Prince?"

"Kind of, I guess. There was one."

"Really? I hadn't realized..."

"His name is Benji. He was taking exams while you were visiting, so you didn't have the chance to meet him." Gabrielle wasn't sure how much to say, but at the same time, she felt the need to share.

"Exams?" asked Edgar.

"Yes, he's in college studying to be a civil engineer. He's very bright. I'm not sure it was the right thing to do. Leaving him, I mean. I don't know now what will come of us." She let the last word hang, half wondering if she could even use the term "us" anymore, as though they were a couple. "It was more like this was something I just had to do, he understood, almost too much, and that was that. "

"Well, they say absence makes the heart grow fonder. You did the right thing...coming here, I mean. It will be good for you. Trust me, if there's one thing I know it's that things always work out for the best. You might not know for a while why you were meant to be here. You're still young; take it from me, once you get to be my age hindsight is the best lesson. The thing is, by the time it becomes obvious, you've already been through a lot." Whether intentionally or not, Edgar sped up the vehicle while he said, "Life is about taking chances. Hang in here with us and you'll see."

Gabrielle felt better. She hadn't known Edgar to be so philosophical.

During his last trip, most of the discussions were with Elodie to iron out the details of the adoption and the move. During his other trips to Haiti there were always friends or family around and they really didn't have the chance to talk one-on-one. There was always a crowd, mostly women, around him. During one trip, Gabrielle had met Stella, Essie's sister, who was the same age as Gabrielle. They had gotten along to the point that Stella shared the family secret with Gabrielle.

"Emmanuel is not Essie's son," she had told her. They were sitting on a wall eating ice cream cones late one afternoon while everyone else was inside.

"Really?" Gabrielle wasn't sure if she should be more surprised by the news or by the notion that Stella felt it was okay to confide in her with the secret.

"Yes, he's the result of a fling. I don't know why my sister tolerates it, but she does. Probably because it's not the boy's fault. She raises him like he's her own. It isn't my business, really."

With those last words from Stella, Gabrielle climbed down off the wall and suggested they check in with everyone inside.

The news of Edgar's affair disturbed Gabrielle, but she also knew that Essie was taking good care of Emmanuel and it mostly mattered that the boy had a family. With Edgar being so much older than Gabrielle, nearly twenty years her senior, she saw him as more of an uncle than a brother. One of the reasons she wanted to come to Germany, to live with them, was that she thought it would be nice to have Edgar around since her own father had been scarce. He and his family would provide normalcy, family. She knew there was some advice he could give, and that receiving it would be good for her. So, she tucked what Stella had told her aside and went with her own instinct about moving in with them.

Chapter Three

WHEN THEY ARRIVED at the apartment building, Gabrielle discovered that Edgar and Essie's apartment was in a high-rise and was on a floor with only a few levels above them. With her luggage loaded, Edgar and Gabrielle rode the elevator to their floor. As they walked down the hall to apartment number 854, she grew anxious to see Essie and Emmanuel. She also couldn't wait to unpack her bags and settle in. That would be the first step toward the normalcy she was craving.

When Edgar flung the front door open, Emmanuel looked up from the table where he was sitting.

"Come on over and give a hand, Emmanuel," Edgar said. "Meet your sister, Gabrielle, and show her to her room. Essie!? Are you here?"

Essie came from down the hall toward the front door. "Welcome!" she said and held her arms out to Gabrielle.

"Hello," Gabrielle said to both of them as they approached. She gave Essie a hug and rubbed Emmanuel's head with her free hand.

"I'll take this to your room for you!" Emmanuel grabbed ahold of the largest piece of luggage and started pulling it down the hall. At just eight years old, he was strong like Edgar, and he even had Edgar's gait.

"How was your trip? Long?" Essie asked.

"Yes, a bit. It feels good to stop moving," Gabrielle said. She looked at Essie, grateful to be in their home.

"Well, let's show you to your room so you can unload your things, then come have a cup of tea and rest a bit before dinner."

Essie led Gabrielle to her bedroom, which was half way down the hall, past Emmanuel's. Gabrielle could see that Edgar and Essie's room was at the end of the hall.

"Thank you, Emmanuel," she said, looking at where he had placed her luggage, now on the floor next to the dresser. He stood in the doorway, grinning. There was a full bath across the hall from her room. She wasn't sure if she would be sharing it with Emmanuel, but assumed so since she didn't see another one. The bedroom was about the same size as the one in Haiti she had just left. One twin bed framed the corner, while another was centered against the wall in the middle of the room. A long, white dresser stood on the opposite wall, and a desk in the last corner made it all very welcoming. When Gabrielle walked over to the window, she saw that the view looked down to the parking lot, but she could also see for miles, being so high up.

"We'll leave you to unpack and get settled. I'll put some water on for tea," Essie said. "C'mon, Emmanuel, leave Gabrielle to get settled."

The door closed and for the first time, a sense of newness hit Gabrielle hard. She knew she was with family, but suddenly the reality that she wasn't in Haiti overwhelmed her, surprisingly so. Until now, Germany had been an illusion, a dream that would come true "someday soon." Now, as she looked at her packed bags on the floor and her new bed, it was real and there was a sense of lost anticipation with an unknowing of the future. Her mother would no longer be cooking her favorite dinners. Benji would no longer be picking her up to go to the movies. The pillow she would lay her head on tonight would probably feel too soft or too hard, too big or too small. Gabrielle felt a vacuum of emptiness fall over her. She sat down on the windowsill, looking out to the vast country and its inhabitants that she knew little about. What have I done?

On the plane, Gabrielle was a stranger to everyone around her en route to a new beginning. Here, she wasn't a stranger, but everything was inherently new, and suddenly she felt frightened. She walked over to the bed in the center of the room, sat down on it, and put her head in her hands with her elbows on her knees.

"God grant me the serenity to accept the things I cannot change; courage to change the things I can, and wisdom to know the difference." She felt a sensation of warmth over her and embraced the feeling as God's love protecting her. In that moment, she felt a shift and shook off the fear, knowing it would come back, but at least for now, she managed it.

I

HOT TEA, EVEN in the middle of summer, was just what Gabrielle needed. Essie handed it to her in a tall, green mug, and Gabrielle's grip on it managed to ground her somehow. She looked around the living room as she sipped slowly from the rim of the mug. There were a few family photos on a table in the corner, taken at various ages and seemingly different locations. With Edgar being in the army, they had traveled to many countries. Gabrielle stood and went over to pick up a picture. Emmanuel must have been about two in it.

"I love this photo. Emmanuel, you were so cute and little," she said, smiling at him. He was back at the table working on a puzzle.

"He was a pistol at that age," Essie said.

"I bet." Gabrielle put the photo down, but not before she looked closer at it, noticing a bruise on Essie's arm. The bruise looked to be a few days old, healing with the yellows coming through. She glanced across the room at Essie, then back at the photo. Seeing it gave Gabrielle chills. Seeing blood or bruises on people always shook her up. She used to joke with Sasha that she would make for the world's worst nurse because she would always be fainting.

"More tea?" Essie asked.

"No, thank you though. I think I'll go unpack a bit more. Let me know if you need help with dinner though."

"I'll call you when it's about ready. You can make the salad," Essie answered.

"Can I come help you unpack?" Emmanuel asked Gabrielle.

"Emmanuel, leave her to her privacy," Essie scolded.

"I won't be long," Gabrielle promised him.

There was a row of hangers in her closet and contact paper in each drawer of the dresser. The clothes she brought with her didn't begin to fill either, but at least by the time she unpacked she started to feel as though she was settling in. The finishing touch was a framed photo of her and Benji that she placed on the nightstand on the left side of the bed. It was taken by Sasha last Christmas, and was one of the very few pictures of herself she had. Her mother was not one to use a camera, and despite—or perhaps because of—her stunning looks, Gabrielle's friends rarely took photos with her. But Sasha had taken the time to capture Benji and Gabrielle that Christmas afternoon—before she even knew she would be going to Germany.

AS GABRIELLE BEGAN to tour the area, she noticed that there were several other tall buildings, and many apartment buildings. Edgar had told her in the car ride from the airport that there was a little shopping center with some small local shops that sold specific goods, like a meat market, a small grocery store, and a bakery, of which Gabrielle would soon learn that she didn't care too much for German pastry. There was a small boutique clothing store where Essie shopped for special occasion clothes. Gabrielle noticed that Edgar's face lit up when he spoke about the public place, a pedestrian area where they had different cultural events, such as festivals, farmer's market, arts and crafts shows and other seasonal activities. He assured her there was plenty to do; it was just a matter of walking out the door and finding it.

Gabrielle had a natural draw to children, so Emmanuel took to her right away and encouraged her to come along with him to town. He prided himself in being able to show her around. She liked having a younger brother around, even though he was already proving to be a bit of a handful. During dinner he protested his vegetables, but sat up and ate them, although reluctantly, when Edgar made it clear there would be consequences if he didn't. He fought going to bed by eight o'clock, stating that he was too old to be going to bed so early. But, Edgar put his foot down and Emmanuel usually snuck a book or a puzzle into his room. Gabrielle once noticed the quick passing light of a flashlight shining under his door, but said nothing.

A few hours after her arrival, Edgar announced, "I have to be at the base tonight, Essie. Won't be back till tomorrow afternoon. Why don't you bring Gabrielle over tomorrow to go shopping? I added a few things to the grocery list, and she might need some clothes or toiletries."

"I'm okay for now," Gabrielle insisted.

"We'll go over anyway," Essie replied. "I'm sure there will be something you need, and we'll get some groceries. I can show you around."

"Okay," Gabrielle said as she ate her last bite of potato. "Thank you for dinner. I hadn't realized how hungry I was, especially for a home cooked meal."

"This is your home now, so get used to the good cooking, and to helping out with it." Edgar stood from his seat, left his dishes for Essie to clear, and went down the hall to their bedroom to change. Ten minutes later he came out, gave Emmanuel a pat on the head and told him to listen to his mother and Gabrielle. He then waved a hand and went out the door. Gabrielle watched for a moment as Essie cleared his dishes and put them in the sink. A moment later, she stood and cleared her own dishes.

That night the pillow proved to be a bit too firm. She tried scrunching it up to soften it, but it never molded to her head the way hers at home had. She wondered if she should have brought it on the plane with her. After tossing and turning until two o'clock, she finally fell asleep with her last thought wondering what Benji was doing.

I

ESSIE, GABRIELLE, AND Emmanuel piled into the station wagon the next morning and made their way over to the base. Essie pointed out notable places along the way while Gabrielle looked out the window and took it all in. She was happy to be out and about rather than being in travel and unpacking mode. The weather was cooler than what she was used to in Haiti, but still rather warm. She wore a sundress and sandals and held her purse in her lap as Essie maneuvered through the base to the shops.

Once inside the shop, Emmanuel saw a friend and ran over to talk to him. Essie made her way through the aisles, picking up the items Edgar had listed as well as ones she wanted. The store was filled with women pushing carts with kids in tow. Gabrielle was a bit overwhelmed at first, but once she got her bearings she was able to figure out where things were and what she might need. She noticed a few men in their uniforms, but for the most part it was women and their children.

"I'll just be over here," said Essie. "If you need anything just holler."

"Okay," said Gabrielle. She continued to make her way up and down the aisles, not looking for anything in particular, but for what she might need that she hadn't thought of. Having left a lot of things behind in Haiti, she was certain something would stand out.

"Excuse me," said a gentleman in his army grub. Gabrielle looked up and came face-to-face with one of the most handsome men she had ever seen. "You look a little lost. Just wondering—do you need help?" he asked.

Taken aback by his approach, Gabrielle took a moment to respond, and when she finally did all she could say was, "I think I am finding everything I need." She blushed at the simplicity of her answer and was surprised by her reaction to this man. She wasn't quite sure what to make of him. It wasn't that she hadn't had men pay attention to her before, it was just that it was this man in uniform standing right in front of her, and for some reason it startled her.

"Okay, just wanted to make sure you're finding everything you need. You are new here, aren't you?"

"Yes, I am. If you know Edgar, he is my brother. I am here living with him and his family." Gabrielle was a little surprised that she gave away that much information to a stranger, but she assumed she would eventually be meeting plenty of other men on Edgar's base. She had a feeling everybody knew everybody around here.

"Ah! So, you must be Gabrielle. Edgar has told us about you. He's been excited for you to arrive. Well done, welcome to town. You're a long way from Haiti, but we are like family here and I'm sure you'll fit in just fine."

"Thank you. I appreciate that," Gabrielle said. She turned down the aisle and walked away so he would not notice her blushing. She also didn't know what else to say. While she was friendly and outgoing with people, she still preferred to maintain her privacy.

A few aisles over, she ran back into Essie, who already had a cart full of groceries.

"Can I help you with any of this?" Gabrielle asked.

"No, I think I have everything." Essie started heading toward the checkout. "Oh, on second thought, you can go find Emmanuel for me. He should be over on that side of the store." She gestured toward the back of the store.

"That I can do." Gabrielle made her way back to where she had just come from, looking for Emmanuel in each of the aisles. When she finally found him, he willingly went with her back toward the checkout line. As they turned a corner in the next aisle, Gabrielle noticed Essie paying for the groceries. When she and Emmanuel approached, Essie asked her to take the groceries to the car and said that she would be right out. Without questioning her, Gabrielle took two bags and handed Emmanuel one bag and together they left the store toward the car. Fifteen minutes later, Essie came out to the car, got in, and put her purse on the floor behind her seat. Gabrielle noticed that Essie had to squeeze her purse between the seats in order to place it on the floor. It was only in the back of her mind that she questioned why the purse seemed fuller than earlier. She concluded that Essie must have forgotten something and ran back inside to get it.

Once home, Gabrielle helped unload and put away the groceries before retreating to her bedroom for some private time. She had moments where she was overwhelmed with missing Benji, and in those moments she turned to her poetry as her salvation. With her favorite pen in hand, she took out her journal and sat down on her bed. When it came to Benji and writing poetry, the words usually just flowed. Today was no different.

Without You

Tonight all nature seems to share my nostalgia
The light wind caressing the trees
Whispers gently in my ear
But I can only hear words of sadness
The sky is grey and the stars are hiding
The birds maintain a stubborn silence
And refuse to sing
Like me, their hearts seem to suffer
The absence of their loved ones
Everything is calm
Suddenly, the sky begins to cry
And sitting on this bench
My tears and the rain unite
My lips try to sing a love song
My heart calls out your name
My soul is tormented
Unable to express my feelings
I let my tears speak
I let my heart whisper to you
That without you, without your love
My life is empty

Gabrielle let the poem sink in. When she was done, she placed the journal and pen on her nightstand, and lay back on the pillow that was too hard compared to the one at home. Slumber engulfed her like a wave crashing on the shore.

I

BY THE END of August Gabrielle had grown accustomed to her new lifestyle and living in Germany. The school year was still to come. Just as she had grown used to a new sense of normalcy, another change laid before her. But in the case of starting school in a few weeks, she looked forward to being among peers her age and the start of her last year of high school. Essie made certain that both Gabrielle and Emmanuel had everything they needed. They had made several trips back to the base shops where they picked up school supplies and new clothing. Coming from Haiti, Gabrielle had no winter clothes. Heading into the fall and winter, she was in need of sweaters, jackets, scarves, gloves, and anything else that might keep her warm in the coming months.

"The fall is a beautiful time of year here, but winter comes in quickly once fall is done," Essie told Gabrielle while clothes shopping. "Make sure you have enough clothes that are school appropriate."

"I am excited about starting school, but also a bit nervous."

"I'm sure you will fit in just fine," Essie said as she glanced sideways at Gabrielle, looking her up and down.

The shirt Essie was holding up would most definitely look better on Gabrielle, and suddenly Gabrielle felt guilty for being tall and beautiful. To add to it, she was slightly taken aback by Essie's tone of voice. In the past few weeks, Gabrielle had noticed a change in Essie's attitude toward Gabrielle, to the point where she was starting to wonder how welcome she was in their home. There were times Gabrielle wasn't sure if she was more of a burden than a blessing to them. However, she did all she could do to help out around the house, and especially with Emmanuel, who proved to be a bit of a handful at times. If it weren't for Edgar and Emmanuel, she would be more concerned. However, it was all the more reason that she was excited for school to start so she could be with teenagers her age and out of Essie's way.

Sometimes when Essie went shopping, Gabrielle stayed home with Emmanuel and played games with him. On those days, she was always a little surprised when Essie came in with several shopping bags, noticing that they seemed to be the same ones time and time again. From the arguments Essie and Edgar often had, Gabrielle had an understanding that they really couldn't afford for Essie to be buying items that she really didn't need. Although Gabrielle never really saw what was in the bags, she knew they weren't essentials, like groceries, because she always took them straight back to their bedroom. Over time, it seemed like the more Essie went shopping, the more goods came home with her. Gabrielle had always been naturally observant of other people and their behavior, but this puzzled her.

Edgar also traveled frequently, and over the first few months, Gabrielle noticed a trend, to the point of being predictable, where the tension between him and Essie escalated leading up to his trips. When Gabrielle knew Edgar was heading out of town again, she intentionally took Emmanuel out for a long walk so they would be away from the arguments.

It was during these walks when Gabrielle learned more about Emmanuel. He was very sure of himself, and even came off as a little bit of a know-it-all. Although the family hadn't been there all that long before Gabrielle arrived, he took pride in being able to show her the ropes. He explained things to her, some of which was common sense to her at her age, and some of it was about the area and things she needed to know. He had a touch of confidence that bordered arrogance, much like his dad, but more tame, and there was something a little bit endearing about it in an eight-year-old. In some ways Gabrielle was impressed that he could be so confident. She knew that Emmanuel never knew Essie wasn't his mother. Gabrielle could certainly see where he took after Edgar, but not Essie. Even still, Essie treated him as her own.

"Doesn't it take a long time to make all that jewelry?" Emmanuel asked. They were on one of their afternoon walks and he was holding one of the bracelets Gabrielle had made. She took it off for him to look at while they walked. Essie had told her over breakfast that Edgar was going out of town that evening, so Gabrielle took it upon herself to get Emmanuel out of the house while Edgar was packing. For the most part, Essie did Edgar's packing for him, but he always had a few last minute items that he wanted to include. It was during those times when the arguments tended to erupt, and Gabrielle had learned to get out before they started.

"Yes, some pieces take a little bit of time. But the better I got at it, the faster each one went. If you want, I can teach you how to make a bracelet. Maybe you can give it to your girlfriend?"

"I don't have a girlfriend! Yuck!" Emmanuel laughed, but was still rather dramatic with his response, which left Gabrielle laughing too. She thought about how the only times she seemed to laugh since she arrived were when she was having these kinds of talks with Emmanuel. Edgar was always coming and going from the base, and Essie seemed to only shop, cook, and watch soap operas. While Gabrielle liked to shop, it wasn't something she could do every day, mostly because she was without money to spend. She didn't understand how Essie could spend so much time in the store, but she tended to stick to her own beliefs about privacy and didn't prod.

The next weekend Gabrielle would find out exactly what was happening. She and Essie were in the store while Emmanuel was with Edgar and his friends. The boys were outside playing games on the field nearby, while the women were mostly inside shopping.

"Open your purse," Essie said to Gabrielle without looking her in the eye. Instead she was looking around and behind Gabrielle. "Don't ask why, just do it."

Gabrielle was surprised, but didn't question the instructions given to her, as she normally would have. There was something about Essie's tone of voice and the way she was looking around the store that told her she better not question anything. Gabrielle held open her purse, and the next thing she knew Essie was stuffing a blouse in it.

"Close that tight, real quick," said Essie.

Gabrielle, shocked, didn't know what to do other than hand the purse over to Essie. She didn't want to touch a purse that had a stolen blouse inside. Essie continued to look sharply around the store, and then shoved the purse back in Gabrielle's hands.

"Shhhhhhh."

"What are you doing?" Gabrielle asked. "I don't have the money to buy this blouse, and I'm sure as heck not going to steal it."

"Gabrielle, it's about time you learned how things really are around here." Essie had started walking down the aisle, as though she was leaving the scene of the crime.

"What do you mean how things are? I don't steal. It's wrong."

"Will you keep your voice down? We're going to get caught if you keep talking so loud. When we get to the end of this aisle, you go left and I'll go right. I will meet you out at the car in five minutes."

Gabrielle was still standing there holding the purse when Essie turned the corner and went to the other aisle. She was too afraid to open it back up, exposing the evidence. She looked around the store, wondering if anyone had seen what had happened. Knowing she was more certain to get caught if she pulled the blouse out of her purse now, she found herself walking quickly toward the door, unsure of what to do other than leave. Once outside at the car, she sat in the passenger seat and took the blouse out. It wasn't even her style. She tossed it over to Essie, who was sitting in the driver's seat shaking her head.

"What just went on in there?" Gabrielle demanded.

"Haven't you figured it out yet? I figured you had. Every time I came home from shopping, you always gave me a look as if you somehow knew."

"Knew what? That you were stealing? No. I had no idea. But, yes, I have wondered how you could afford to do so much shopping on Edgar's salary. It wasn't my business, though, so I never asked. Now that I do know, I don't want anything to do with this." Gabrielle gestured toward the blouse in disgust. "Does Edgar know this is how you spend your days?"

"Of course not. If I were caught, the trouble he would be in would be unthinkable. Let alone what he would do to me." She shivered. "All the wives do it, though. It started out as a game, but it's more than that now. It's sort of like...well it...you wouldn't understand, but it's like an addiction or an escape. Clearly you're still too young and don't know what it's like to be married to somebody who treats you more like a servant than a wife."

Gabrielle heard a quivering in Essie's voice in those last words. She was starting to see the toll being married to an army man was taking on Essie, but it still did not make stealing right. She looked over at Essie and said, "Edgar is a good provider, and you're risking his entire military career by getting a thrill out of stealing? He has been nothing but good to me, and from what I see, other than your arguments before he goes away, he's good to you and Emmanuel."

Essie started the car without saying a word. Gabrielle looked out the window toward where all the men and boys were playing in the baseball field. She didn't want to know Essie's secret. She didn't want to know that her sister-in-law was betraying her family by stealing. Without thinking much more about it, Gabrielle opened the door and climbed out of the car before Essie started driving. Without looking back, she slammed the door shut and walked over to the baseball fields. When she approached the men, she noticed that they all turned her way, looking at her quizzically. Emmanuel ran over to greet her, and Edgar waved from across the field. She didn't know what she was going to do about her newfound knowledge, but she knew that in that moment she needed to be with the boys and not feel the need to fit in as one of the girls.

A few hours later Edgar, Emmanuel, and Gabrielle walked back in the apartment. Essie was in the kitchen chopping vegetables with more vigor than usual. Edgar took no notice when Essie only gave them a glance over her shoulder, but Gabrielle knew that shoulder was a cold one.

"We're back!" Emmanuel said. He sat down on the couch to kick his muddy sneakers off.

"Don't you kick mud on the carpet, Emmanuel! Clean that up then go wash up for dinner. It will be ready in about twenty minutes," she said. "Gabrielle, set the table for me, please."

Gabrielle noticed that the word please was emphasized as more of a command than a request. She pulled the napkins and silverware from the dining room buffet and laid them out on the table. In the kitchen, she took three glasses from the cabinet in the corner and filled Emmanuel's and her glasses with milk and Essie's with water. For Edgar, she retrieved a cold beer from the fridge. Preferring it right from the bottle, he didn't use a mug.

The tension had grown so thick, not even the steak knives on the table could cut through it. Gabrielle was relieved that Edgar didn't seem to notice the friction between Essie and her. With Emmanuel enthusiastically telling Essie about their day on the baseball field, he had no idea what a saving grace he was right then.

As Gabrielle took her last bite, Edgar said, "Gaby, how about you come down to the base with me tonight. Some of the guys and I are going to shoot pool. You can hang out."

"That sounds great," Gabrielle said.

"What about...," Essie began.

"What?" Edgar asked.

"Nothing." Essie stood from her seat, and all they saw of her from then until the moment they left was her back as she stood at the kitchen sink doing dishes. Gabrielle felt a tang of guilt for not helping with the dishes, but at the same time, Edgar was ready to leave and she didn't want to cause a problem with him.

THERE WERE FOUR pool tables in the pool hall on base and about as many men there to play per table. Relieved to be out of the house, Gabrielle was glad to be sitting amongst the group of men. She didn't know a thing about playing pool, other than hitting the balls with a stick in hopes of sinking them in a pocket. It didn't matter though; she was enjoying watching them play.

There was a big, comfortable couch against the wall between a set of two tables. Gabrielle sat down with a soda and some chips. Some of the men stood around the tables, propping themselves up with their pool sticks. A few sat on stools at the bar, and one sat on the arm of the couch awaiting his turn.

"Edgar, your turn," one of the men on a stool said. Edgar was at the bar getting another beer.

"Coming!" he called. The other men stepped back from the table so he had plenty of room to position himself. Stick alongside his body, he took his time eying the ball and the intended pocket. Gabrielle listened while the strike of the stick against the ball and the clamor of the ball against other balls echoed sharply around the room.

"Nice hit," someone said as he came in through the door. Gabrielle turned her head and immediately recognized the man as the one in the store a few weeks back. She felt her face flush as she instinctively crossed her legs. Not wanting him to see her flushed face, she looked back toward Edgar's table.

"Seat taken?" he asked.

It took a moment for Gabrielle to realize he was talking to her. "Uh, no. Please..." She caught her right foot bouncing slightly up and down and immediately stopped the motion.

He sat down next to her and smiled. "First time down here? Pool hall, I mean?"

"Yes, Edgar brought me down. Do you play?" Gabrielle asked. She suddenly felt childish holding a cola instead of a beer.

"Oh, he plays all right," Edgar called from across the room. "Pool isn't all he plays though..."

The room broke out in laughter. Edgar stood tall, seemingly pleased with his joke. But, Gabrielle knew that Edgar's underlying purpose was not to evoke laughter from the men, but to warn her to stay away from the handsome man who just walked through the door.

"His name is Peter. Peter, that's Gaby, my sister," Edgar said with an emphasis on sister.

"Don't you have some balls to play with?" Peter asked. More laughter erupted, and Edgar did indeed go back to his game, but Gabrielle noticed that he kept one eye on her and Peter and the other on the pool table.

"So, your name is Gaby? Cute," he said.

"It's Gabrielle. Only family calls me Gaby." Gabrielle didn't mean for the words to roll off her tongue the way they did.

"Gabrielle. Lovely name, and it's nice to meet you. Can I get you another drink? What do you have there? Rum and Coke?"

"No, this is just...how about a beer?" Gabrielle knew Edgar would not approve, hoping he might make an exception or wouldn't notice, but both were a long shot.

"One beer coming up." Peter made his way to the bar and put money down for two beers. The bartender looked over at Gabrielle, who smiled back. He popped the caps off and handed the two bottles to Peter. Gabrielle watched as he made his way back. He was in street clothes this time, rather than a uniform, and wore jeans and a lightweight sweater that was tight enough to outline his physique. Gabrielle couldn't help but notice how fit he was. His natural build was broader than most of the other men, making him stand out. He had brown curly hair and green eyes, but it was his smile that kept making her blush. It too was broad and very genuine.

Her guard was up though. Even though it had been a few months since leaving Haiti, she had been writing to Benji daily. Edgar would mail the letters for her, and every time he came home with the mail, she looked to see if there was a personalized envelope amongst their bills. The one time there was, it was a card from her mother. While she was happy to hear from Elodie, there was a part of her that was disappointed.

"Here you go," Peter said.

Just then Edgar made his way over to the couch. "Peter, she's too young to drink that. Soda is all she gets tonight."

"Edgar, I can handle just one—"

"I said no." And with that he walked back over to the pool table.

"Sorry, Peter. Maybe the bartender will trade it out for a soft drink?"

"That's okay, I'll drink both. But let me go get you another soda."

When Peter returned, they sat on the couch and watched as the others played pool. A few of the men asked Peter if he wanted to join in, but he just shook his head and said, “No, not tonight. I’m enjoying just watching.”

They only occasionally spoke when someone made an exceptional shot on the pool table, yet Gabrielle felt a sense of security having Peter sitting next to her. At times, her mind drifted off to Benji, but she did her best to stay present in the moment. It’s not that she was looking to date other people, but there was something about Peter’s presence that made her realize it could be a possibility someday.

It was around half past midnight when Edgar came over to Gabrielle and announced it was time to go home. The entire night he had kept that one eye on the pool table and the other on Gabrielle and Peter. It was the first time that Gabrielle had been around the men on base in front of Edgar, and she could feel his unrest with the situation.

“Good night, young lady,” Peter said.

“Good night, and thank you for keeping me company.” Gabrielle ran to catch up with Edgar, who had taken one more look over his shoulder to ensure she was coming along.

The drive home was a quiet one, and when they walked in the door, it was evident that Essie had already gone to bed. Their home was quiet, but the tension remained.

Chapter Four

DURING THE FEW weeks leading up to school, Essie came home with new clothes for Gabrielle. She would bring one or two items at a time, and Gabrielle could only assume that they were not paid for. They never again discussed what happened that day in the store, but Edgar made it clear to Essie that he wanted Gabrielle to have new clothes for school. The clothes were always left on Gabrielle's bed, and everything but one pair of pants fit. At Gabrielle's height, it was hard for her to find pants that fit, but Essie couldn't have known this. Gabrielle never mentioned that they were too short, and decided those would be the pants she would wear with tall boots. She wasn't accustomed to dressing for the warmer weather, and was actually looking forward to wearing sweaters, long skirts, boots, and pants. It was the bulky jackets that she didn't look forward to as much.

The army base was in the town of Mannheim, which was also where Gabrielle and Emmanuel's school was. On her first day at the Mannheim American High School, she and Emmanuel walked together to his school, then she continued on a few more blocks to hers. She had already been by several times over the summer and went once for a tour a week earlier. Mannheim American High School was primarily for the children of the military, and since their apartment building had several military families in it, there were many kids who also walked to school that day. German families lived in their building as well, but those children attended other schools in town.

The classrooms themselves were universal; it was how days were spent on the inside of the classrooms that distinguished one school from another. Gabrielle had always been one of the best students in her class in Haiti, something that she strived for and worked relatively hard to earn. A natural intelligence helped, but she was one of those students who studied, not only for the grades, but because she enjoyed learning. Knowing she would go far with her education, she anxiously looked forward to graduating and starting college.

But for now, she stood in a long hallway, looking at the numbers on the rows of doors in search of

Room 25, her homeroom. When she found it, she opened the door and nine pairs of eyes fell on her. The teacher's back was to the classroom as she wrote in big letters across the board, "Mrs. Carter." Underneath she added a long sweeping line.

The other universal law of schools had been defined by the few eager teacher pleasers sitting in the front row. Mrs. Carter turned around by the time Gabrielle sat down and smiled at her when she saw that Gabrielle had taken a seat in the front row alongside two other students. The rest sat in the rows behind them.

Just as the bell rang, a group of three students, two girls and a boy, bounded through the door. Like a chain link, the boy walked between the two girls, who each had their arm strung through his. They made their way to the third row and sat down in unison next to one another.

"Next time be in your seats when the bell rings," Mrs. Carter said.

"Yes, ma'am," the trio sang out, also in unison.

As Mrs. Carter went into her first day of class introductions, handing out of the syllabus, and expectations of behavior and contributions, the class took it all in, or most of it.

Gabrielle felt like she was in a time machine being in an American classroom in Germany. She listened closely to Mrs. Carter and occasionally looked at her fellow students when they asked questions.

When Mrs. Carter introduced her to the class, she simply said, "I want you all to welcome Gabrielle, who is here from Haiti. It's not easy coming into a new school your last year, so please welcome her and show her around."

Several students said, "Hi Gabrielle," and smiled or nodded at her. Not normally so, she was caught off guard by her sudden shyness. She chalked some of it up to feeling like an outcast. As Mrs. Carter pointed out, it was their last year, and most of these students had spent at least one year, if not more, together. Now at the pinnacle year of school, they were ready to wind down and move on next spring. Gabrielle was certain that inviting a new student into their fold at this point was seemingly irrelevant. At the same time, they still had many months of school to go, and she hoped to make a few friends. However, her main focus was on earning honor roll grades that would land her in a reputable college.

By the end of the school day, Gabrielle had attended five classes. She ate lunch alone in the cafeteria, mostly because nobody invited her to eat with them. Most of the teachers she liked; the one she didn't care for as much was her math teacher. Thinking about the year ahead in the math class reminded her of when she first met Benji and how he helped her and Sasha with their homework. Just one more thing for her to miss about Haiti and Benji.

THAT NIGHT AFTER dinner, Edgar invited Gabrielle to go back to the pool hall with him, but she declined so she could get a jumpstart on her homework.

"Just as well, Peter will probably be there tonight, and we don't need him buying you any more beers."

Edgar was sitting on the couch reading the paper and the comment went without his raising his eyes from the columns on the black and white pages.

"That was just that once, and I didn't drink it," Gabrielle said. "It's not like I'm not almost old enough anyway."

"Almost is the key word there, Gaby." He turned the page of the paper and flicked it into place.

Edgar was the only one to call her Gaby, other than her mother. There were a few times when Gabrielle caught the look on Essie's face when he spoke to Gabrielle, who wasn't quite sure how to interpret the expression. Edgar and Gabrielle talked about their days during dinner, when they could get a word in edgewise between Emmanuel's stories. Essie, on the other hand didn't have much to contribute, and Gabrielle often found herself looking for anything to talk to Essie about just to make her feel included. Edgar didn't seem to notice that she was more often than not left out of the conversations, and most nights he went back down to the base after dinner, either to work or to just hang out with the guys at the pool hall.

It was after observing Edgar and Essie when Gabrielle often thought about what life would've been like if she had stayed in Haiti and married Benji. Would they have eventually grown apart the way Edgar and Essie had? She believed not. It was something she often reflected upon. Not so much the marriage part, but the growing old together part.

Later in her bedroom, she sat down and wrote a letter to Benji about her first day of school. She caught herself trying not to sound like a young schoolgirl, but the maturing woman she wanted him to see. Their youthful romance and young, sweet love would have eventually blossomed into a mature relationship. She thought often about her desire to give him her virginity on their wedding night, that magical night when everything in the world would be perfect and her joy and happiness would defy any description. It hadn't been anything they discussed, but she certainly thought about it and imagined that he had too. She felt in her heart that one day she would return to Haiti and they would have that opportunity to be together as one. The year ahead of her was about her being able to grow into the woman that she felt she needed to be for them to take that next step.

Dear Benji,

School has begun and it is a relief for me to be back in an environment where I can be challenged intellectually again. I am counting the months until spring when I graduate. Some days it seems like forever from now, and others it seems like right around the corner, if you count wintertime as a corner.

Fall will be here soon. I will be excited to see the leaves change and eventually fall from their trees. Emmanuel says he builds piles of leaves to jump in, but I cannot imagine what that must be like. Winter will be a challenge, but I have bought some sweaters, boots, and am practicing tying scarves around my neck.

I often think of you and wonder how your own studies are going. Are you on an internship yet?

Studies are calling, so I must tend to them. I wish you could help me with my math!

I miss you, my love,

Gaby

When she finished writing, she sprayed a tad of perfume on the letter itself, folded it neatly, and put it in the envelope that she would address with his name on it. When the stamp was securely placed, she tiptoed down the hall and left it on the counter for Edgar to mail the next day.

THE FOLLOWING WEEKS were busy for Gabrielle with settling into school, a fair share of homework, and adapting to the change of seasons. Summer seemed to transition to fall quickly while she was inside the walls of the classrooms. Despite being several weeks into school, not one student invited her to eat lunch with them. They often asked her for help with homework before or after class, but that was the extent of their interactions. She usually brought her books with her to the cafeteria and sat at the table against the far wall where she essentially blended in with the plaster. Not even the teachers took notice of her sitting alone. The upside in her mind was that she was able to finish her own homework, and if she didn't have much, she would bring a book to read.

I

IN THE MIDDLE of November, during dinner one night, Edgar surprised Gabrielle by telling her he wanted to teach her how to drive before the snow falls became regular.

"Really? I can learn to drive?" She was very excited to be reaching this point in her life. She understood that it came with responsibilities, but it also came with the freedom that she craved. Of course she wouldn't be able to afford a car for a while, but when that day came, she would already be a good driver.

"Sure, you are old enough now. We can go out this weekend," Edgar said.

"Can I go?" Emmanuel begged.

"Of course not," said Edgar. "But, you can eat the rest of your vegetables." Edgar pointed at Emmanuel's plate with his fork.

"Oh, geez," said Emmanuel. "I don't get—"

"Emmanuel, you heard your father. That's enough," said Essie.

Emmanuel stuck his fork in his vegetables and feigned interest in eating them.

THAT NIGHT, GABRIELLE was anxious to write to Benji once her homework was done.

Dear Benji,

You will never guess the news I have to share! Edgar is going to teach me how to drive. We start this weekend. I dream of someday being able to take a Sunday drive with you, love. Wouldn't that be wonderful?

My classes continue to go well, even math. Although I certainly work harder to earn my good grades in there.

It paid off because I earned all As for my midterm grades. Time to start looking at colleges, don't you think?

The fall air smells so clean and crisp, probably because it is so much drier than the humidity in Haiti. When I leave for school in the morning, the cool air nips at my nose and cheeks. The ground is usually covered in frost at that time of day, but it melts away by midmorning, especially when the sun is out.

The classrooms are bright, but sometimes damp and hold an aroma of chalk dust that makes me want to sneeze every morning when I walk in the door.

Speaking of school, I must get some sleep now. The alarm goes off early!

I miss you, my love...

Gaby

Gabrielle folded the letter and went through her ritual of sealing and addressing it. What she had left out of her letter was the fact that she ate her lunches alone in a small section of the cafeteria. It was a far cry from the days when she and Sasha ate lunch or did homework together after school.

GABRIELLE HAD NEVER made any promises to Benji about when she would return to Haiti. When they were together, they chose to live in the moment and not ponder too much over the future. But, in her mind, Gabrielle spent time in the future. She just knew that someday she would return to see her Benji.

IN EARLY DECEMBER, a new student named Donna transferred to their school. Donna was an African American girl and on the first day of her arrival, she sat down in the front row right next to Gabrielle.

"Hi there, I'm Donna," she whispered to Gabrielle.

"Welcome. I'm Gabrielle. It's great to have you here," Gabrielle responded.

From that moment on they became best friends who tried to help one another with the cultural differences, and what each one knew already, they shared with the other. Relieved to finally have someone to eat lunch with, they sat with their heads together while they ate and talked. Within a few days, Donna introduced Gabrielle to Sarah, a Korean girl who actually lived Gabrielle's apartment building. They had all felt like outsiders, and when they could, they met after school and did their homework together. Gabrielle's first quarter grades were just barely her usual straight As, which frustrated her. She had struggled more than usual to earn them, and she didn't want Donna and Sarah to think that was her typical academic level. However, the more the three studied together, the more Gabrielle started feeling confident in her studies again. Sarah was a whiz at math and Donna had a knowledge base about history that impressed Gabrielle. They quickly learned one another's strengths and weaknesses and focused their studies around them.

I

"ARE YOU READY?" Gabrielle heard Edgar call to her from the hallway.

"Almost!" She was excited for her third driving lesson. They had found a country road outside of town that was perfect for her to practice on. Edgar had proven to be patient with her behind the wheel, especially the first day when she had no idea what she was doing.

"It's normal for the pedals to feel clunky and the steering wheel to seem overly responsive," he had told her. Within an hour, however, she had a good feel for it and from there on out it was more about anticipating what to do next with what lay ahead of the vehicle and on the road.

"Okay, I'm ready," said Gabrielle as she came out of her room. She wore tall brown leather boots, jeans, and a blue wool turtleneck sweater. She found, especially at her taller height, that this look was rather appealing and a nice change from the sundresses she was used to wearing year round. She had seen pictures in magazines of women wearing fall and winter clothes, but of course never had reason to wear them herself until recently.

They were soon in the station wagon heading down the road, Gabrielle in the driver's seat and Edgar in the passenger seat. He occasionally pointed to an upcoming road and told her to take this route or that route. He had her practice stopping short, taking sharp turns, and anticipating unexpected happenings along the road.

"Pretty much the only things that could come at you unexpectedly out here would be some form of wildlife running out in the road," said Edgar. "Just keep watch."

He also kept on point and told her about what to expect when it started snowing, how the roads would be more slippery, and how on the hillsides drivers still had to keep the car moving in order to keep the momentum going.

"A lot of people think you have to go really slow in the snow on the up hills, but the truth is you need some momentum so you don't slide backwards," Edgar explained.

"That makes sense," said Gabrielle. She watched the road intently, but acknowledged all that Edgar told her. The sun was starting to set and streamed through the windshield into her eyes.

"Of course if it's icy, there's nothing you can do. But you won't be driving on that anyway. I think we've done enough for today, let's head back home."

They were only gone for a while that day before returning home where she went back to her bedroom to finish her homework.

"It's more important that she gets her homework done and pulls in good grades," Edgar had told Essie when school started. He was ensuring that Essie let up on Gabrielle having to help as much with kitchen duties once school was in full session.

By now they were heading toward the holidays, and Gabrielle was busy studying for exams and writing papers. She didn't go to the pool hall with Edgar quite as much, except on the occasional Sunday afternoon when her homework was complete and after doing some housework to keep in good graces with Essie. Sometimes Peter was at the pool hall, and he remained friendly toward her, but by December most of the men knew well enough that Gabrielle was off-limits. Edgar made sure they understood that. On the one hand, Gabrielle appreciated being looked after by him. She felt he was providing her with the benefits of the father figure she had been seeking. On the other hand, there was a part of her that liked the attention from the men and she didn't want to be so overprotected.

"Do either of you ever get attention from any of the men on base?" Gabrielle asked Donna and Sarah one day at school during lunch.

"Yes, I do. I find that a lot of the men are very nice, and for the most part respectful," Donna said. "But, I haven't had any of them blatantly ask me out or anything yet. What about you, Sarah?"

"Who me? I still have the body of an eight-year-old boy; most men don't pay attention to me. However, there is one in particular that I talk to. He's only twenty years old. I don't see him very often, but when I do we have some very interesting conversations. He's really quite smart, and I enjoy talking with him."

"Oh come on, Sarah, you're going to be absolutely gorgeous one of these days," said Gabrielle. "Just you wait and see; it's always the shy late bloomers who suddenly one day turn heads and everybody wonders what the heck happened."

Sarah laughed and closed the textbook she had open on the table. "Well, I hope you're right."

"Is that all we had for homework?" Donna asked. "If so, I need to get home and help with dinner." They were working in the school library rather than at one of their houses. They liked going there after school because it afforded them some privacy to talk away from their homes where parents' hovered. Even still, they each had to be home in time for dinner.

They packed up their books in their backpacks, and when they left the library, Donna turned left toward her house while Gabrielle and Sarah walked home to their building. They said good night to Donna, and said that they would see her at school the next day.

"Any plans this weekend?" Sarah asked as they approached their building.

"Nothing yet. I'm hoping I can go for another driving lesson. I love them because they give me a sense of control. You know?" said Gabrielle as she pulled the large glass door to their building open.

"My parents won't let me take lessons until next spring. We're not sure where my dad will be stationed next, so they use that as an excuse not to teach me to drive on one side of the road or the other." Sarah pushed the Up button and they waited for the elevator to arrive.

"I guess that makes sense, but it does sort of sound like a copout," said Gabrielle. They stepped into an empty elevator. "Hopefully you can start lessons in the spring though."

The elevator door opened and Sarah exited on her floor.

"See you in the morning," she said.

Gabrielle waved goodbye and watched as the elevator door squeezed close again.

That night Gabrielle wrote a letter to Benji, and for the first time, told him of the new friends she had made. She wondered if he would question why she never mentioned friends until now, but she couldn't over analyze it. In all of her letters, she wanted him to feel connected to her. It had been five months since she left Haiti, and she still hadn't received one letter from him. She conjured excuses for him in her mind, such as that he was uncomfortable writing letters or that he didn't have the money to buy a stamp or that he was simply just too busy with school and starting to look for a job. The reality of the lack of correspondence hurt more than she was willing to admit, and making up excuses seemed to appease her. But nothing kept her from writing letters to him and placing the envelopes on the counter for Edgar to mail when he went to the base each day.

Gabrielle had broken the habit of checking the pile of mail every day when Edgar came home. She would still glance at him when he walked through the door, hoping that he would announce that there was a letter for her. But that day hadn't come, and Edgar had never questioned all of the outgoing letters. He would, however, ask her if that was all she had to mail. She would reply yes, and out the door he would go. Sometimes he teased her for the smell of perfume that exuded from the envelopes or the heart she would draw on the outside. But, he never discouraged her from sending them or suggested she should stop. Gabrielle appreciated that. And even after all this time, she still hoped that one day an envelope would come through the front door with her name written on it and a postmark from Haiti.

Chapter Five

RAISED BY HER grandmother until she was five, Gabrielle's mother had left them behind in order to go to the capital city, Port-au-Prince, where she could work toward gaining the financial resources needed to properly take care of and raise Gabrielle. It wasn't until Gabrielle turned five when Elodie was able to return and begin raising her.

Elodie knew her mother had done the best she could with Gabrielle, but it was also time for Gabrielle to start school, which meant an entirely new level of responsibilities. Immediately wanting to do what she could to make up for lost time, and always wanting the best for her daughter, Elodie took the advice of a friend who highly recommended one of the reputable all-girl Catholic schools. She was more than overjoyed and proud when Gabrielle was accepted, as it helped make up for her previous absenteeism. If she could at least help Gabrielle get her schooling done right, she would feel successful as a mother.

What Elodie hadn't expected was that she now had a rather feisty five-year-old daughter on her hands. While living with only her grandmother, Gabrielle had become very accustomed to being spoiled. By that age, she had become the kind of little girl who had no problem speaking her mind, often to the embarrassment of her mother. There were times when Elodie became overly stressed with Gabrielle's feistiness, even to the point that she tried to restrain Gabrielle's spunk by pouring cold water over her head. That only irritated Gabrielle more. Their battles were ongoing and when the time came for Gabrielle to attend her new Catholic school, Elodie worried about sending her outspoken and free-willed daughter into the hands of nuns; hands that she knew carried long rulers and weren't afraid to use them on children. At the same time, she secretly hoped the nuns would help straighten Gabrielle out.

"You be good for those nuns," Elodie told Gabrielle over and over.

"I will!" Gabrielle tried to reassure her as best as a five-year-old could. With Gabrielle's continuously uncontrolled behavior at home, Elodie had no reason to believe her; however, she knew time would tell...and that the nuns would take care of her.

Elodie never alerted the nuns of Gabrielle's tendency for outbursts. Instead she chose to observe, and to her pleasant surprise, Gabrielle proved to be very well behaved in the classroom, and wholeheartedly embraced the school's structure and her teachers. Besides being an avid reader and eager learner, earning her the spot as a favorite among the nuns, Gabrielle was quick to make friends, and not just because students wanted her help with their homework, but because she endeared people with her shy smiles and warmth. Gabrielle proved herself to be a different child in the walls of the school compared to the walls of her home, and Elodie hoped that one day the same behavior would carry over to their home front.

Because Gabrielle took kindly to the nuns, she adjusted to her new learning environment more readily than most of the other students. Elodie relaxed as the first year moved along, and eventually she got to the point of being very proud of Gabrielle. By the summer when Gabrielle turned six, she had thrived in her first year of school, had spent the school year living with her mother, and was ready to spend that summer with her grandmother until school started up again in the fall.

Even the Catholic schools in the Haitian school system inherited the French school system from French colonization. First grade through eighth grade were known as the primary school grades. At the end of eighth grade there was a national exam that each student had to pass in order to move on to secondary school. The students who passed their exams received a certificate that allowed them to enroll in secondary school, which consisted of their ninth through fourteenth years. After the completion of that thirteenth year, they took a national exam and moved to the fourteenth year. After the completion of the fourteenth year, they took their last national exam that represented the completion of school. At the time when Gabrielle left Haiti, she was only halfway through her fourteenth year, her last year before college. She hadn't completed her fourteenth grade because she left in July and school wouldn't start again until that fall.

From the time she entered school until the time she moved to Germany, Gabrielle left her own special footprint on the Catholic school's landscape. She set a high bar for students around her, and everyone knew it, but oddly, none of the students were jealous or resentful. They tended to go to her for assistance instead. Through these years, her leadership role took on an organic beginning, and as she grew, she knew that someday she would hold a leadership position.

In typical Catholic school fashion, the nuns were very strict; they didn't refrain from using corporal punishment to maintain discipline and to punish those who didn't get good grades. In order to keep the school running smoothly, they had to apply very stringent disciplinary rules. Each morning the girls started their day with a general assembly in the school courtyard. Every class lined up according to height with the shortest ones at the beginning of the line, and because of her height, Gabrielle was always at the back of the line. Ensuring that all the students respected the dress code, the teacher for each classroom inspected the girls' uniforms, which comprised a white shirt, a blue and white checkered skirt, black shoes, white socks, white or blue hair accessories, and clear short nails. The Mother Superior—the Director—led the Morning Prayer, followed by the girls saying the Pledge of Allegiance and singing the National Anthem of Haiti, La Dessalinienne. The last order of the morning assembly was when the Mother Superior delivered a brief message that was often a word of encouragement followed by school announcements. It wasn't until then when the teachers and their classes were dismissed to their respective classrooms.

The classrooms were rather basic, with each desk containing a built-in chair and a small, rectangular compartment for school supplies. The students began their day with their homeroom teachers, and throughout the day all of the other teachers came into the same room to teach different subjects. This reduced the need for students to gather in or go up and down the hallways between classes. Even though the teachers were very strict, Gabrielle found that some of them were also kind. Some of the teachers were nuns; some of them were laywomen. Each student was expected to earn a certain average grade for each subject, and if they failed to achieve this level, they were subject to receiving a certain number of licks with the wooden ruler. They also had a system where all students were ranked first, second, third, and so forth in their class. These rankings were determined monthly and quarterly, and those students who ranked first wore a medal of honor for a week.

By time Gabrielle and her classmates had their first few school years behind them, they began to settle into a routine. Fortunately for Gabrielle, she was also motivated by her love for books and thirst for knowledge, which was an advantage over many of the students. Gabrielle earned good grades, and before long she ranked very high in her class. She consistently ranked first or second every month or quarter, which made Elodie even more proud when her daughter wore the medal home.

DUE TO HER ongoing success in school, Gabrielle had become quite competitive with maintaining good grades. At the same time, Elodie did her best to create a good home environment. Their daily routine became familiar, and was actually quite simple since Gabrielle rarely strayed from school, homework, dinner, and going to bed. Elodie didn't want Gabrielle to be distracted, so she forbade Gabrielle to play with the other kids in the neighborhood. Being an only child, and though she made friends easily, Gabrielle's interaction with other children was limited to her fellow students and only during school. School became the center of her world. All of this contributed to her early development of a strong thirst for knowledge. She excelled in almost every subject—except math. Because of this, there were several years when Elodie enlisted Gabrielle's math teachers to tutor her during lunchtime in order to ensure she kept up. Not only during lunch, but afterschool, too, Gabrielle spent her time reading, writing, and studying. It was no wonder she always ranked first in the class.

"Gabrielle, would you like to answer that question?" The teachers would often ask. Gabrielle rose to the challenge, knowing the other students wouldn't snicker, but were instead relieved that Gabrielle was called upon instead of them. She tended to bail them out of potentially embarrassing situations of giving the wrong answer, let alone a snap of the ruler on their wrists if they were wrong or came off as being snarky. Because of the strict discipline in the classroom, Gabrielle saved disciplinary action toward many students by answering with the correct response. During test taking, no one dared to try to cheat off of her, but they often crowded around her in the hallway afterwards asking what the answer was to particular questions. Sometimes they smiled because they knew they got the question right, and sometimes they frowned and cringed because they knew they hadn't done so well. Through all of this, Gabrielle earned and maintained a leadership role that would carry her through her school years.

DESPITE ELODIE'S STRINGENT social rules, Gabrielle still managed to make friends. They played during recess, which came daily after lunch, and those were the times when she truly felt like a child, laughing and playing. There were also days when tutoring took up much of recess time, but on the days when the math teacher let her out early and in time to enjoy what was left of recess, she played hopscotch in the courtyard or huddled on the stairs and just talked and giggled with her friends.

By the time Gabrielle was done with sixth grade, she had done so well in school that Mother Superior suggested that Gabrielle skip seventh grade. Elodie burst with pride when Mother Superior called her into her office with Gabrielle.

"The school doesn't do this often, but I'd like to recommend that Gabrielle go straight to eighth grade at the end of the school year." At the time, Gabrielle was completing her sixth grade year.

As proud as she was at first, Elodie had to ask, "My only concern is that the eighth grade is known to be a very pivotal year because of all the preparations for the national exam. Naturally, this is very important. Are you sure she will be suited to perform as well in school and pass the exam?"

"I understand your concern, and I can assure you that Gabrielle will receive any extra help she might need to compensate for the gap," answered Mother Superior. "Her teachers will be well aware of the transition and you know you can always come see me if you have any problems during the school year."

All the while, sitting in her own chair, Gabrielle was beyond excited by the vote of confidence from Mother Superior. This gave her wings and motivated her beyond words. She worked very hard during her sixth year; she stayed focused and continued to receive tutoring in math, and now all of her efforts were paying off. When the time came and she took the national exam, she passed with flying colors and agreed with her mother that she should continue on to secondary school at the same school.

It was during the first few weeks of her eighth grade year when Gabrielle made friends with a classmate named Sasha. Gabrielle was relieved that Sasha already had a circle of friends who took her into their fold. Until meeting Sasha, Gabrielle was focused on her studies and hadn't tried too hard to befriend anyone, especially since she still had her own friends; they just weren't in the same grade anymore. However, one of them was already a friend of Sasha's, which was how they ended up meeting.

On one particular day during lunchtime tutoring, her math teacher asked, "Does it bother you that you're here rather than playing with your friends?"

"Some days it does. However, when I get a test back, I can tell my mom that I earned an A, which spares me the repercussions of earning a lower grade! That's when I remember why it's worth being here."

He laughed and they continued working on the next problem.

I

BY THE TIME Gabrielle turned ten, Elodie was in a serious relationship with a man named Jacques. Elodie had been through many tumultuous relationships up until then, but things quickly settled down when Jacques came into her life.

Though Gabrielle was too young to understand the situation, Jacques was married and courted several mistresses on the side, Elodie being one of them. At the time in Haiti, there was an unspoken acceptance of polygamy, and even though he was married, it didn't take long for Elodie and Jacques's relationship to grow into more like husband and wife than married man and his mistress. Jacques was very vocal, both in their home and on the street about Elodie being his favorite.

Jacques' wife knew of Elodie, but she showed not a care, nor did she make a fuss about it. Theirs was a marriage of convenience, not love. Jacques had two daughters with his wife, and was known to have fathered several other children with other women. Each of the other women knew that Elodie was his heart's true desire, and they accepted it as long as he continued to provide for their children.

With a man consistently around their home, Gabrielle noticed that Elodie treated him like a king. He came home to Elodie nightly, and the ritual was that she would set his bath water, warm up his dinner, bathe him, and listen attentively as he talked about his day. He was a supervisor at the City Hall in Port-au-Prince, and Elodie would listen closely as he told tales, all the while feeding him with food, attention, and adoration.

Gabrielle usually retreated to her bedroom to do homework and didn't build a strong relationship with Jacques. But she remained respectful, for she saw how much her mother loved him. He never filled the shoes of any sort of father figure, nor did he have any say in the matter about how Elodie raised Gabrielle, but he was always supportive of Elodie's decisions. When

Gabrielle left for Germany, Jacques said goodbye to her in a non-emotional way, which fell in line with how Gabrielle had perceived their relationship for the past seven years.

During the time while Gabrielle was around Jacques and her mother, she had learned more about what she didn't want in a relationship than what she did want.

"Mother, I know you are his favorite, but he still has all these other women. How are you okay with that? Why would you even be okay with that?" Gabrielle asked one day. She was only about fourteen and just starting to think about relationships. She believed in her dreams of having her own success in life, and not counting on a man to support her. But, when it did come to love, she held on to the fairytale of having her one Knight in Shining Armor. Even if her mother had chosen to have many knights, and finally settled for one who also had many princesses, to Gabrielle, her fairytale relationship still had plenty of time to come to her. She held to the truth that it would.

To answer Gabrielle's question, Elodie explained, "Gabrielle, adult relationships are complicated. You will learn someday that there is no perfect 'one.' You are still young though. For now, stay focused on school and don't worry so much."

Gabrielle let the words skim over her mind, not accepting them as her own. After that, she never broached the subject about Jacques again. He and Elodie continued on with their relationship and Gabrielle continued on with school and friends. If anything, she appreciated the sense of calmness around the house that his presence brought. The fact that he made her mother happy was enough for her to accept it all, even if her young mind couldn't wrap its head around it. And when she finally left Haiti, she actually hoped that Jacques would be there to take care of her mother.

Chapter Six

IN THE DAYS when Edgar was out of town, Gabrielle would bring in the mail. Every trip to the mailbox had become a trip to a world of disappointment. Every step toward the mailbox had been a step of hope, of anticipation that that day would be the day when her sweetheart would come to his senses and say, "Yes, Gabrielle, you are the one I want."

So on one Thursday afternoon when Edgar walked through the door with a stack of mail and tossed one of the envelopes onto the table in front of Gabrielle, her heart raced. The first thing she noticed was that the postmark was from Haiti.

“Looks like he finally responded,” said Edgar with a smirk.

Gabrielle didn’t take the time to respond to him, but rather ran down the hall to her bedroom with the envelope in hand. She closed the door and sat down on her bed. Her hands shook as she tore open the envelope and pulled out a folded piece of paper.

“Dear Gabrielle, I’m sorry I haven’t written sooner. It’s been very busy here. But I was thinking about you, and wanted to write.”

Gabrielle’s stomach sank when she glanced down to the bottom of the letter and saw the signature as Sasha’s. Her eyes scanned back to the first paragraph as she continued to read what Sasha had to say, consciously looking for any word of Benji. It wasn’t until the third paragraph where Sasha wrote the devastating words, “You should know that Benji has someone in his life, and it’s serious.”

Gabrielle felt a flash of heat fall over her. She fell back on the bed and stared at the ceiling. Void of an immediate reaction, she lay there in shock.

How could he? But she knew that wasn’t a fair question, as they had no formal commitment.

Who is she? But she knew that it didn’t matter. Whoever she was, she wasn’t Gabrielle.

Gabrielle had always believed there to be a silent understanding between her and Benji that it would always just be the two of them, that at some point they would find their way back to one another. She had even told him so when they bid their goodbyes at the airport.

Suddenly her mind began to swirl with thoughts, doubting everything, most especially her choice to leave him. Seeking some kind of answer, any answer, she continued reading the letter, bracing herself for what would come next.

"I believe he may have started seeing her before you even left, but he won't give me any details. I always wanted you two to stay together forever because I loved not only both of you, but how the two of you were together. All I know now is that the word marriage has come up a couple of times in passing conversations, and I thought you should know. I don't know if you have heard from him, as he has not mentioned anything. Have you written him?"

Gabrielle burst into tears.

What have I done? She believed she was doing what was best by coming to Germany, and as it turns out she could have lost what was always truly the best thing for her. She turned over and cupped her pillow around her face in order to muffle her sobs. Even still, there was a knock at her door.

"Are you okay in there?" Edgar asked.

"Yes," Gabrielle mustered up the best possible 'yes' she could under the circumstances. It didn't work, however. Her door opened slightly, and Edgar stuck his head in it.

"What did that boy say to upset you? I've never seen you this upset."

"The letter isn't from Benji," Gabrielle said as she wiped her eyes as dry as she could. By now she was sitting up on the bed holding her pillow tight to her stomach as though it would keep her from throwing up. Edgar came in the room and sat down on the end of her bed.

"Then who is it from? Elodie?"

Somewhat reluctantly, Gabrielle responded. "No, it's from Benji's sister, Sasha. I really don't want to talk about this right now."

"Well, I haven't said anything yet, but day after day I have been mailing letters to this boy for you, and you haven't received any responses." Edgar's tone had shifted from concern a moment ago to commanding. "It's about time you stopped embarrassing yourself and move on with your own life. Whatever's going on with him now doesn't have anything to do with you anymore. You are living here now. This is your life."

Even though Edgar had spoken a bit harshly, there was a small part of Gabrielle that knew he was right. But there was still that bigger part that believed that she and Benji were meant for each other...only each other. The thought had never crossed her mind that there might be someone else, especially not this soon, let alone the notion that he was seeing someone before she even left. The ache she was feeling stretched from her stomach to her heart to her throat, feeling like a rope tightly pulling the three organs together.

In order to appease Edgar, and in hopes that he would leave the room, she simply said, "I know you are right. I will feel better tomorrow; it will be another day."

Those words seemed to work, as Edgar stood up and made his way to the door, but not without saying one last thing. "Whoever this Benji boy is, all I know is you are too good for him. And if I ever meet him, I will tell him just that." With that, Edgar left the room and closed the door.

Gabrielle reached down to her journal and pulled out a letter she had written to Benji just the night before. She had planned on finishing it that night.

Dear Benji,

I am starting to worry that I haven't heard from you. I feel as though maybe I have let you down, but I want you to know that you are the only one for me. You are who I think about when I lay my head down at night, when I think about having a husband and a family. It's always you...

Gabrielle tore the letter in half and tossed it on the floor. Not wanting to look at it, she lay her head back down on her pillow and stared at the corner of the room where two walls met until she was called for dinner.

She didn't read the rest of Sasha's letter that night, but instead folded it and put it back in its envelope. At some point she would respond to Sasha, but for now she had to let the reality of losing Benji to someone else sink in.

During dinner Gabrielle poked at her vegetables with her fork, only managing to swallow a few of them down.

"Gabrielle, you need to eat your dinner. Whatever's going on doesn't mean you can't eat." Edgar was increasingly firm in his tone. He hadn't addressed Gabrielle that way before. She had heard him use that particular tone with Essie and Emmanuel, but never her. Taken aback, she pitched her fork into her carrots and took a few more bites. Several moments later, Edgar stood to leave for base.

"I'll see you all tomorrow," said Edgar as he pulled on his jacket and left.

Once the door closed behind him, Essie asked, "What is going on?"

Since Gabrielle and Essie had formed the distance between them, she didn't really care to open up to her, but at the same time she needed someone to talk to.

"The letter was from Benji's sister. Apparently he has met someone new...," the rest of Gabrielle's words got caught in her throat and she couldn't finish the thought. "If you don't mind, I'd like to go to my room. I'm sure I have some homework to do. If you need me to, I'll do the dishes later before bed."

"Well, that's too bad. I'm sorry to hear that." Essie's words, while seemingly caring, cut deeply at Gabrielle's heart. She knew Essie wasn't sorry, and more likely than not was secretly happy that Gabrielle had been hurt.

"I'll be okay," said Gabrielle. "I have plenty of good in my life. My friends, school...and you all. Things always happen for a reason. God will see me through this. He has to." Gabrielle felt compelled to assure Essie that she would land on her own two feet, and by going the extra step to recognize their family as part of the good in her life, she diffused Essie's jealousy.

At the same time, Emmanuel sat silent as he looked up at Gabrielle with wondering eyes. Gabrielle saw that he was worried, and said, "I'll be okay, Emmanuel; don't you worry about me."

Gabrielle stood and cleared her dishes, taking Edgar's with her. She laid them down in the sink and ran some water over them, but did nothing more.

"As I said, I will do the dishes later," Gabrielle assured Essie before walking down the hall. A moment later the only sound in the apartment was the closing of her bedroom door.

Later that night, when Gabrielle came out of her bedroom, the lights were off except for a small one in the dining room that was left on for Edgar when he came home. Gabrielle tiptoed into the kitchen, noticing that Essie had already done the dishes. Gabrielle imagined that rather than out of compassion for Gabrielle, Essie had done them so that Edgar wouldn't be mad if he came home and saw them in the sink. She would never know for sure, but it was true that dirty dishes left in the sink triggered his temper.

After retrieving a tall glass from the cabinet, Gabrielle opened the refrigerator and pulled out the carton of milk. From the cookie jar, she pulled out three cookies and with milk and cookies in hand, she sat back down at the dining room table. She didn't turn on any other lights, as she wanted to be in as much darkness as she could. There was just enough light to see the snack in front of her, and that was enough.

Each cookie was carefully dipped in the glass of milk followed by a small bite. Between bites, she stared at the half-burned candle on the table. The candleholder was brass and stood only about six inches tall. There were two of them, but the other was at the other end of the table. They had been a wedding gift to Essie and Edgar. Essie told her that the first night Gabrielle had arrived, now several months ago. Gabrielle couldn't remember who gave it to them, but had noted that the holders were one of their nicer gifts.

While Gabrielle stared at the wax where it had hardened and dribbled down the side of the candle in streams, she thought about all the times in the past several months when she wondered where Benji was and what he was doing.

The image of him holding hands with someone else, going to the movies, taking long walks, and anything else he might be doing with another woman, had never once crossed her mind.

She only imagined that he had been sitting there in Haiti missing her and thinking about their times together as much as she had been doing the same in Germany. She pictured him leaning against their tree reading her letters and missing her, wishing she would come back home. But this new reality, the one where somebody else was in his life, had not been in the story she had told herself. Gabrielle had written Benji letters nearly daily since she had arrived, and even came to terms with the fact that he never responded. But now, knowing what she knew, she was uncertain if she should continue writing to him.

There were times when Gabrielle kept Edgar in the dark about how often she was truly writing letters to

Benji. She would save them up and mail them herself at the end of the week. Most of the letters contained poetry that was both to him and about him, but several of the letters also let him know what she was doing in Germany. The tone of the letter depended on her mood; oftentimes she wrote poems if she was missing him, and other times she wrote a newsy letter if she was having a better day.

For some reason, these were the ones that she would leave on the counter for Edgar to mail from the base.

Every day, however, she had hoped that Edgar would walk through that door with a letter from Benji in his hand. There were times when she wondered if Benji had written her, but perhaps Edgar was hiding the letters from her. But Sasha's letter confirmed that not only did Edgar give her the letter, but that Benji had moved on and had not likely sent her any sort of letter. She knew she would never know at this point if Benji had done so without actually talking to him.

I

THE NEWS THAT Benji was dating someone else, and likely before she even left Haiti, continued to wreak havoc on Gabrielle's emotions. With the holidays ahead of her, she felt empty and alone, even amongst her family. Christmas came only a few weeks after the letter from Sasha had arrived. Gabrielle had been too distraught to write her back, but finally decided to send Sasha a Christmas card. She didn't mention Benji or the letter, only wished her a Merry Christmas and said that she would touch base again after the New Year.

The turmoil Gabrielle was feeling only added to the already uncomfortable situation at home with Essie. Between the emotional overlay that clouded over her and the ongoing tension between her and Essie, Gabrielle was beginning to feel like she was in a prison, both physically and emotionally.

When Christmas came, there was very little excitement even though Edgar brought home a Christmas tree and the four of them decorated it with ornaments and white lights. Essie hung simple stockings in the dining room since they had no fireplace.

It seemed as though there was an unspoken truce called between Gabrielle and Essie since the night of Sasha's letter. Gabrielle was relieved by the ease in tension, but also wondered if it would resume after the holidays.

During the week leading up to Christmas, she and Gabrielle baked cookies and bread to go with their turkey dinner. Although this wasn't the typical Haitian meal for Christmas Eve, Edgar insisted on it, so Essie complied.

No one from the outside was invited over, and Edgar continued going to the pool hall most nights, except for Christmas Eve and Christmas night.

There were a few presents under the tree for Gabrielle and Emmanuel, but only a few since there was not enough money for splurging. Gabrielle wondered if Essie backed off on shoplifting around the holidays, as though the guilt may have gotten to her. Essie and Gabrielle only exchanged one gift each. Emmanuel opened the most gifts of them all, which was fine by

Gabrielle. She had already lost the one gift she wanted the most. No present in the world, other than Benji showing up on her doorstep, would have made it a truly Merry Christmas.

Since Gabrielle and Emmanuel didn't have school until after the New Year, they found time to be with their friends. However, all of the extra, unfocused time didn't help Gabrielle's mindset. She kept busy reading books and taking walks, but she missed Christmas in Haiti, which was much more exciting.

In most cases, Christmas Eve in Haiti actually took precedent over Christmas itself. Everyone was anxiously excited, not sleeping while they waited up for Santa Claus to arrive. They stayed up late, cooking their special Haitian holiday dish of fried pork with rice and red kidney beans. Along with it, they made Pikliz, a shredded cabbage dish used to spread over the fried pork. They also indulged in fried plantains, which were green bananas.

Christmas was a magical time in Haiti with the lights, all of the children, and all of the festivities. To top it off, everyone attended midnight mass. Gabrielle had asked Edgar and Essie a few times since she arrived if they could find a church to attend. The first time she asked was the second Sunday after arriving when she noticed no one mentioned it or was getting ready to go. She asked Edgar, who answered with, "I'm a good Catholic, but I don't need to spend my Sunday morning in church. It's my only day of rest around here."

It wasn't until around the middle of November when Essie and Gabrielle were grocery shopping when Gabrielle brought it up again.

"Oh, no," replied Essie. "We went once to the service on base when we first got here, but we didn't care for it."

Gabrielle never asked again, but she had expected they would at least make an exception for Christmas. The topic never arose, and it turned out to be a very different Christmas in cold and gloomy Germany, where the only festive view was from the lights in the stores that they could see down below from their apartment. There were no activities on the base for the children, and everyone seemed to stay to themselves. It was by far the gloomiest Christmas Gabrielle had ever spent.

With more time on her hands, and not sure whether or not to write to Benji, Gabrielle spent more time writing in her journal, as she did on Christmas Eve.

The holidays have been especially hard for me. Everything is different here compared to Haiti. It's lonelier and depressing here without all of the festivities that Christmas brought in Haiti. Worst of all, I can only imagine what Benji is doing with whomever he is with now. I try not to think of them exchanging gifts...or worse yet, other things.

God, where is the serenity I pray for?

Chapter Seven

EDGAR AND GABRIELLE continued her driving lessons after the holidays ended, but only on days when snow wasn't falling. It was a Sunday, and being a sunnier winter day than most in February, the roads were clear and dry. Essie and Emmanuel had gone out with friends, and it was early afternoon when Edgar suggested they take another drive.

"Grab your things," called Edgar from the hallway. "Let's go out for a drive while the others are out."

"Okay! I'll be right there," called Gabrielle from her bedroom. "Hold on for one second."

Gabrielle leaped from her bed, excited to escape the apartment and to take a break from homework. She went over to her dresser and pulled out a pair of warm wool socks to exchange for the light cotton pair she was wearing. Already dressed in jeans and a turtleneck sweater, she grabbed a scarf out of the closet and wrapped it around her neck before pulling on a black wool coat.

"Ready," she said as she came down the hall. She gathered her hat and gloves from the closet next to the front door and pulled those on as she followed Edgar out the door and down to the parking lot.

"I have a new route planned for today. It's one you haven't driven yet. It gets a lot of sun, so the snow melts quickly. We can go that way. I'll give you directions."

Edgar climbed in the passenger seat while Gabrielle took her place behind the wheel. About five miles into their usual route, Edgar instructed her to bear left instead of right at the upcoming fork in the road. Gabrielle was relieved to have a new route to change the scenery and roadways up a little bit.

"Go up here about two more miles," said Edgar. "There is a huge lake with a pretty view. I bet it looks nice this time a year." Edgar fidgeted with the glove box as he spoke, fishing through papers while keeping one eye on the road ahead.

Gabrielle drove along, paying close attention since it was all-new to her. It had been dry for several days, so the trees' branches were bare of snow. However, the snow alongside the road was hard-packed with tall snowbanks in various places.

"This is so much prettier than the other way," Gabrielle said.

"Less talk and a little more driving," Edgar said. "Go about a half mile up here; it's on the right."

"Yes, sir." Gabrielle was confused by his change in tone, but kept driving and didn't question it.

As Edgar had indicated, a half mile later there was an opening to a large, shimmering lake. The lake was beautifully covered with snow for as far as Gabrielle could see. The surrounding trees and woods were untouched, still displaying the pure white snow from the last snowfall. There were no footprints or tire marks in sight, making everything magical to view. The sky was a brilliant blue in contrast to the white, iced over lake. The glare of the sun angled down on one side and only a few fluffy balls of clouds floating above the far end of the lake.

"Pull in here and park in that small parking area up there on the right."

"Can we get out and take a look around?" Gabrielle asked.

"Of course. That's why we're here. So you can experience the beauty." Edgar closed the glove box one last time, pulled on his gloves that had been sitting on the dashboard, and tightened the green and blue plaid wool scarf around his neck before opening his door.

Gabrielle shut the engine off and climbed out of the car. As she stood looking out at the lake, the scene before her and the cold air quite literally took her breath away. She could hear Edgar closing the door on his side of the car and the crunch of the snow beneath his boots as he made his way around to the driver side.

"Sure is beautiful, isn't it?" he asked.

"Yes, it—" Gabrielle started to speak, but a wool glove suddenly covered her mouth, gripping it tightly. She felt Edgar's knee push against the back of her own knee from the side. She had yet to close the front door and between losing her footing and a forceful push with his left arm, Gabrielle fell back into the driver's seat.

Edgar's scarf dangled down in her face as he straddled her and pressed his body on top of hers. She frantically looked around, uncertain at first of what was going on. In the next moment, his other wool glove began to tug fiercely on the button of her jeans. Gabrielle looked up at her brother with wide, frightful eyes. Only her left leg seemed to have any ability to move under his weight, so she forced it up toward his groin. Instinctively, Edgar heighted his stance so that her knee couldn't reach his groin. The muscles of his legs squeezed with force against her legs to keep them still, and with a tightened grip on her wrists, he kept her from being able to wiggle out from under him.

Gabrielle's attempts to scream were muffled by his wool glove, which was now damp alongside her top lip from her nose breathing down on it. She felt a strong burning sensation on her wrists from the friction of the wool gloves bearing down on her. In that moment, as the cold air bit at Gabrielle's hips, Edgar pulled her jeans down around her knees. Now with his other hand pressed tightly between his legs, he was able to pull it out of its glove, using his one bare hand to unbutton his own jeans.

As Gabrielle lay there staring up at Edgar, shuddering in disbelief, he only looked straight ahead and out the passenger window. His scarf still dangled in her face, agitating it and causing her to shake her head to the side, her only ability to move on her own. No sign or any form of explanation came from Edgar when she attempted to look in his eyes—nor did he look down at her, not once.

Suddenly she felt Edgar press into her. Her body and breath seized from the agonizing sharp pain. Her eyes squeezed shut and her body went limp.

It was then when Gabrielle went deep inside her mind. She intuitively shifted gears, as though she switched over to some sort of subconscious autopilot where she suddenly found herself back in Haiti with Benji leaning against their favorite tree. Benji was standing beside her, stroking her hair, and telling her how beautiful she was. She could see him smiling at her with not only his mouth, but with his eyes. The color of hot chocolate, his eyes always consumed her. She felt the warmth of the sun as it laid its rays upon them while they stood there. He plucked a petal off the early spring bloom from their tree and handed it to her, telling her that she was his blossom. She hugged him close, feeling every beat of his heart.

"PULL UP YOUR pants!" Edgar demanded.

Gabrielle came to, gasping for air. Shocked back into the reality of the situation, she was no longer in her happy place in Haiti. Instead, she was facing her own flesh and blood; the man who had just violated her innocence. Trembling, and in excruciating pain, she did as she was told and slowly zipped up her pants and buttoned them. She noticed a stickiness inside her jeans that was damp and cold against one of her legs.

"Get in the passenger seat." Edgar stood back two steps and waited for Gabrielle to get out of the driver's seat.

Pulling from the energy the sunlight provided, Gabrielle climbed into the passenger seat, relieved to have some form of escape. Once in the seat, she sat trembling both inside and out. Her only relief was that the strength of the sun warmed her as it streamed in through the windshield, landing on her face. At the same time, a draft of cold air blew in from off the water of the lake and sent chills up her spine. Between the two, the tears that had welled up in her eyes had dried before they could fall. She was afraid that if she cried, things would only get worse.

EDGAR STARTED UP the station wagon and began to back out onto the road. Gabrielle looked out the window at the sunrays hitting the ice packed lake. Completely numb, no thoughts went through her head; her mind had become paralyzed with shock. She leaned into the window, with her legs crossed and her knees aimed toward the door. It was her hands that she didn't know what to do with, so they lay limp in her lap.

"You owed me that, you know," said Edgar. "After everything I've done for you, you owed me that." The words floated around the station wagon like vapors. They made no sense to Gabrielle, nor could she absorb them into her consciousness.

Edgar pressed harder on the gas pedal, making his way toward home. As Gabrielle looked out the window, the trees whipped by creating a blur that matched the thoughts that barely started to form. By the time they reached home, it was late afternoon.

"I am going to the base. You go on upstairs. And if you say one word..."

Gabrielle looked over her shoulder at him as she closed the car door. It was the first time she was able to muster up any sense of emotion. She glared at Edgar, who wasn't looking back at her, but said nothing because they both knew there was no way she could tell anyone what he had just done. Instead, she walked in pain toward the front door as he pulled away with the tires squealing.

Once upstairs, she was relieved that Essie and Emmanuel were still out. In her bedroom, Gabrielle removed all of her clothing and threw them in a pile in the corner of the room. She pulled a towel down from the closet shelf and went across the hall to the bathroom where she turned on the shower. While the hot water pushed the cold water through the pipes, she looked in the mirror. In the reflection, she could only manage to look at her face. She didn't want to witness any part of her now naked and violated body.

Still a bit pale from shock, Gabrielle stepped carefully into the shower and stood under the hot water as it streamed from the top of her head down her back. Once soaked, she opened her eyes and looked to see a swirl of blood making its way down the drain, turning almost pink from the water.

Managing to lather the bar of soap between her hands, she started washing her body from head to toe, careful not to rub too hard where she ached and was bruised. Unsure of how long she was in the shower, time had lost all relevance, every nook and cranny had been accounted for by the time she shut off the water. As she reached out to grab the towel, she caught a glimpse of her body in the mirror and winced. Each curve and shape of it had been meant for her Benji, not for anyone else, and especially not for the brother she thought she could trust. The one she saw as her savior during a moment of time when she needed to escape. He had somehow become someone she didn't recognize; someone who she now knew was capable of violation in a way she never could have fathomed.

After Gabrielle dried off, she wrapped the towel around herself and padded down the hallway where she wrote a note to Essie telling her she wasn't feeling well and wouldn't be eating dinner. Gabrielle doubted Edgar would question her about missing dinner, and assumed he would tell Essie to leave her alone. Back in her room, she pulled on a pair of gray sweatpants and a red sweatshirt before climbing into bed. The only thing she could think to do next was to write a poem. She was a bit surprised by how the words managed to flow despite the numbness that had engulfed her.

Escape
Head down
Eyes closed
A scary world
Mouth open in disbelief
Dry lips
Not a sound
Open arms
Clenched fists
No embrace
Chest lifted
Torn heart
The soul in turmoil
Legs apart
Feet hanging
Needless to fight
The law of the strongest prevails
The mind wanders
The body surrenders
And the soul evades
Into the abyss of despair
It's over...

Gabrielle put her journal back in her nightstand drawer and dropped her head to her pillow. Tucking tightly under the covers, the ceiling was the last thing she saw before she shut off the light and fell asleep.

Chapter Eight

"GABRIELLE, GO DOWN to St. Joseph Street and see Jean-Pierre. He has money for me. Just pick it up and come right back."

Gabrielle looked up from her studies to see Elodie sitting on the couch in the living room. Her feet were propped up on a small wooden bench and a glass of iced water nearly dangled from her hand, letting its contents roll up against the rim, taunting the floor below.

"Yes, ma'am." Gabrielle rationed that she needed the break anyway.

Wearing a light yellow sundress, brown sandals, and large hoop earrings, Gabrielle set out into the warm spring evening. She took the shortest route to her destination, stopping only to pet a cat that came out of an alley, purring at her feet.

"Good kitty," Gabrielle said as she bent down and ran her fingers along the length of the cat's body. It was long and thin with orange and black markings. Its matted fur made it difficult to pet. When a car turned the corner, the cat became frightened and scurried back into the alleyway between a dumpster and a wall. Gabrielle imagined most of its food came from the same dumpster.

A few blocks later, Gabrielle knocked on the door of the address her mother had given her. Swirls of cigarette smoke pooled from the gap in the doorway as it opened, only slightly at first.

"JeanPierre? I'm here for Elodie." Gabrielle stood tall outside the door, hoping the money was readily available. The stench of smoke and the dark interior were deterrents alone.

"Right. Come in and have a seat," the man said as he opened the door. He stood back a step, exposing his bare chest, wearing only a pair of blue jeans.

"I'll wait here," Gabrielle insisted.

"It's going to take a minute; come in." His voice was nearly demanding as he gestured her toward the doorway. Gabrielle reluctantly stepped inside. The stench of his body odor repulsed her further as he reached around her and closed the door.

"Have a seat. I'll be right there." He pointed to the couch.

Gabrielle looked around the room. It was dark, but surprisingly tidy. She took a seat on the couch and watched as he sauntered down the hall. While she waited, the only sounds were the ticking of the clock on the wall across the room and a fly buzzing on a light fixture behind her, even though the light was off.

"Tell Elodie this is all I've got," said JeanPierre as he returned from down the hall. He held the money out in front of him. Gabrielle stood and waited for him to bring it to her. When he didn't, she stepped into the middle of the room and reached for it.

"Not so fast, sweetheart," he said with an alarming glint in his eyes. He suddenly grabbed hold of Gabrielle's arm.

"Just give me the money," Gabrielle said as firmly as she could, trying not to show her fright. "Leave me alone!"

"Not until I get what I want, little girl." His breath was hot on her cheek and a spattering of spit landed on her forehead.

Gabrielle snatched the money from his hand and turned to leave when she felt him grab her shoulders. His forceful grip attempted to aim her toward the couch, but with planted feet she pivoted her body toward the door.

"Stop it!" she screamed.

"Shhhh, sweetheart. Just cooperate and no one will get hurt. Be a good girl."

Only two steps away from the door, Gabrielle was able to reach out and grab hold of the door handle. As she held tightly to it, she kicked her right leg backwards, landing her foot in the groin of the man standing behind her.

"You nasty girl!" JeanPierre yelled as he fell to the ground, clutching his groin. Gabrielle swung the door open and quickly stepped out onto the sidewalk before he made it to the doorway.

An old man passing by asked her if she was okay. JeanPierre slammed his front door, and Gabrielle nodded at the old man. "Yes, I am now. Thank you," she said.

"Okay," said the old man. He tipped his head at her and continued walking in the other direction.

Gabrielle heard nothing from inside JeanPierre's home, but her pace as she walked home was much faster than when she headed out not even an hour earlier. She felt her legs trembling as she looked over her shoulder with every new block until she reached her own front door.

"Mom! How could you send me to him? To this...this JeanPierre?" Gabrielle screamed as she came through their front door. "Do you know what he thought?"

"Gaby, dear, are you okay?" Elodie asked, quizzically. "Did he give you the money?" She was sitting in the same spot as when Gabrielle had left.

"No, I'm not okay. Well, wait, I'm not hurt, but I'm not okay either. Do you know what he tried to do? Did you know he would try to do that?" Gabrielle's heart raced inside her chest as fast as her words spewed out. The tone of her voice remained at a contained pitch, but was heightened and implied accusation all the same.

"Gaby, I'm sure you misunderstood him. He's a nice man. Did he give you the money?"

Gabrielle pulled the money out of her pocket and threw it on the couch next to her mother. "There's your money. Thanks a lot!" She turned away and moments later slammed her bedroom door.

THE SLAMMING OF the bedroom door in the dream was the sound that startled Gabrielle out of her nightmare. Breathing heavily, she pulled herself up and leaned on her left elbow. Once her eyes adjusted to the room, she looked around at the window, the dresser, and the door before she realized she was in her bed in Germany, far away from Haiti and a long time since seeing JeanPierre that night. Relieved, she steadied her breathing.

The nightmare had caused sweat to pour out of her body, drenching her sweatshirt and sheets. The moonlight shined through her window, exposing the rim line of snow that had piled up on the windowsill days earlier. Remembering that she was in Germany, not Haiti, she sat upright and shook her head before cupping it in her hands.

The dream had been a flashback to a time of innocence, a time of innate strength, and also a time she would just as soon forget. A brief time in her life when she had trusted her mother and when her world was still pure.

After stretching her arms above her head and letting her heart rate lower, she lay back down on her pillow. Eyes now wide open, she looked up at the ceiling that had become her new focus of attention. She found solace in its blank space as it allowed her to wash herself away into nowhere.

Sometime before sunrise, Gabrielle managed to fall back asleep. When she awoke the next morning, she thought about the dream and remembered that the next morning after her visit to JeanPierre she dressed for school, ate breakfast, packed up her books, and left the house while her mother slept in her room down the hall. That incident became a pivotal moment in her teen years that changed something inside of her forever. The fear he instilled in her and her innate reaction made it evident that from that day forward, everything was different. The way Gabrielle walked; the way she addressed her mother. Everything.

A few weeks later Elodie sent Gabrielle back to JeanPierre to collect more money. While she agreed to go because she knew her mother needed the money, she always waited outside. He never looked her in the eye and always seemed to know when she was coming, as the money was in his hand when he opened the door. No words were spoken, no eyes met, only the exchange of money passing hands.

The nightmare had mirrored each moment as it unfolded, and the reminder on this night—of all nights—held Gabrielle hostage to her new reality. Edgar, her own flesh and blood, stole her innocence right out from under her. Her female intuition had seen JeanPierre coming. It told her to be careful. But, nothing in the world could have prepared her for Edgar blindsiding her. She flinched as she pictured Edgar's cold breath streaming from above his scarf and swirling around her head while he panted—and how her own breath failed her through the pressure of his hand on her mouth.

ON EITHER OCCASION, with JeanPierre or Edgar, Gabrielle hadn't left her room for the rest of the night. Instead, she lay in bed and stared at the ceiling wondering why. How could God let this happen? Back then, she heard her mother moving about the house doing her nightly chores as though everything was normal and nothing happened with JeanPierre. Just hours earlier, she had heard Edgar talking to Essie down the hall, as though it were any other night. Both times, Gabrielle was trapped in the corners of her four bedroom walls trying to make sense of the violations.

I

WHEN GABRIELLE'S BARE foot hit the ground the next morning, she felt a pang shoot up her thigh. The pain forced her to sit back down on her bed. Stiff from head to toe, she managed to stand again and make her way over to the mirror.

Her normally dark brown eyes were blood shot from crying during her sleep throughout the night. There was a bruise on her wrist where Edgar had squeezed too hard to hold her down. In her mind, she suddenly saw a flash of the photo of Essie in the dining room. Her bruises made sense now, and in that moment, Gabrielle ran across the hall and threw up in the toilet.

She kneeled on the ground and pressed her body against the cold porcelain. When the nausea passed, she reached up and pulled down the washcloth from its rack. Without getting off the floor, she reached with her other hand to turn on the cold water in the sink. She let the running water douse the washcloth for a moment before squeezing it and applying it to her forehead.

When she felt like she could stand up again, she gingerly applied toothpaste to her toothbrush and managed to brush her teeth without looking in the mirror. She knew if she did, if she looked in the mirror and saw the tragedy before her, she would likely throw up again. Instead, she stared down at her feet while the toothbrush swept across her teeth.

She looked at her painted toes, the red she had picked out several weeks ago, and thought about how Donna and Sarah each picked the same color. They took their shoes off during lunch one day and painted their toes, which were just dry enough to re-shoe before their afternoon classes began.

She then brushed her tongue, a bit too aggressively, and spit everything out of her mouth with force into the sink where she ran the cold water to wash it down the drain.

The silence throughout the apartment let her know that no one else had woken up yet. It was Monday, and in some regards she was relieved to be able to go to school. On the other hand, a bigger part of her wanted to climb under the covers and only listen to the pounding of her heart while the world around her carried on.

"Emmanuel, you need to walk to school on your own today. I'm meeting some friends before class," Gabrielle called to him from the kitchen. He was sitting at the dining room table eating cereal, his spoon clanking against the bowl every few seconds. Gabrielle poured herself a small glass of orange juice, but didn't have the stomach for food.

Luckily, Essie and Edgar hadn't emerged from their bedroom yet. Gabrielle was trying hard to plan her departure before she had to face Edgar.

Dressed in fuzzy winter boots, blue jeans, and a wool turtleneck sweater, Gabrielle grabbed her jacket, hat, and gloves from the closet and strapped her backpack on her back. She opened the door, looked over at Emmanuel, and said, "Have a good day, kid."

He waved at her and with a mouth full of cereal muffled a goodbye.

Gabrielle had a new perspective about the kind of life both Essie and Emmanuel had been subjected to by living with Edgar. She could only imagine what might have been going on behind closed doors and before she arrived.

It wasn't until she was several blocks toward school when Gabrielle's head caught up with her feet. She looked around and realized how far her legs had carried her, even though she still had a few blocks left before she reached school. Her legs were sore; in fact, her whole body was sore. More than that, a foggy feeling engulfed her.

"Gabrielle! Gabrielle! Wait up!"

Gabrielle turned to find Donna and Sarah several steps behind her.

"We've been calling out to you for blocks," Sarah said, out of breath.

"I'm sorry. Didn't hear you," Gabrielle said as she readjusted her backpack to keep it from sliding off her back.

"You okay?" Donna asked. "You look a bit, I don't know...not like yourself."

"Yeah, I'm okay. I didn't sleep well, that's all," Gabrielle said.

"Did you do the English homework?" Sarah asked.

"No, I didn't get it done. I was busy..."

Gabrielle tuned out the world around her during the rest of their walk to school. She could hear Donna and Sarah talking, but nothing registered.

Several minutes later, Gabrielle clunked her backpack down on her desk and when the bell rang at the end of class, she realized she hadn't absorbed one word Mr. Coleman had said. In the upper left hand corner of the chalkboard she could see where he had written down their homework assignment. She peeled open her notebook and on a blank page that would normally contain well-documented lecture notes, she wrote down the page numbers and exercises due the next day.

"Let's meet in the library after school," Donna said as the three of them walked down the hall to the cafeteria at lunchtime.

"Definitely," Sarah said. "Are you in, Gabrielle?"

"Sure, that sounds fine," said Gabrielle, relieved for the after-school delay in returning to the apartment.

After picking out their lunches, they took their usual table against the wall. Gabrielle moved the mashed potatoes from one side of her plate to the other with her fork, never lifting a bite to her mouth. When the bell rang for their afternoon classes, her paper plate—still filled with food—hit the inside of the garbage can. She was relieved Donna and Sarah hadn't seemed to notice, or if they did, they didn't say anything.

It was during English class when the day caught up to Gabrielle. She was sitting in the front row, as usual, and her teacher was writing a handful of gerund examples on the chalkboard. Gabrielle looked up from taking notes when the room started to swirl. Everything looked like the blending of different colored paints in a can with the swirl of a wooden stick blending them in circles.

Her forehead became damp with sweat; her hands turned cold and clammy. She struggled to maintain consciousness as her pencil dropped to the desk. She could feel the stickiness between her fingers where the pencil had been. Landing on its eraser, the pencil bounced off the desk and onto the floor, landing next to her boots. She closed her eyes, clenched her fists, and felt her body turn lifeless. The sounds of the classroom faded away as though into another galaxy. Light vanished and all she saw were tiny white spots like stars in the dark of night.

"CAN YOU HEAR me? Gabrielle? Can you hear me?"

Light pierced Gabrielle's eyelids. It took a moment for her to realize the school nurse was laying a cold compress across her forehead. She was stretched out on a padded table with a thin white blanket draped on top of her. Although she tried to open her eyes, the fluorescent light shining down from the ceiling aggravated them. She rolled over onto her side and into the fetal position, hugging her knees with her arms. The nurse adjusted the white blanket on top of her, and asked her once again, "Gabrielle, can you hear me?"

"Yes," Gabrielle mumbled with her eyes still closed. "What happened?"

"You fainted in your English class. Reginald and Herbert managed to bring you in here. I've called home, and someone is coming to pick you up." The nurse turned the cold compress over; it had turned warm on Gabrielle's forehead already. "Put this thermometer under your tongue for a moment," the nurse said.

Gabrielle obliged and wondered at the same time if it was Essie or Edgar coming to pick her up. She didn't want to leave school. She wanted to be able to go to the library after classes with Donna and Sarah and pretend like everything was normal. But her body and her mind rebelled against that idea. Normalcy wasn't anything she expected to experience again for a very long time, if ever.

It was then when Donna and Sarah poked their heads in the nurse's office.

"Can we see her?" asked Sarah.

"Only for a moment," the nurse said as she took the thermometer out of Gabrielle's mouth. "She needs her rest. Her family should be here momentarily to pick her up."

Donna and Sarah rushed to Gabrielle's side, each one grabbing one of her hands and holding them tightly. The warmth of their fingers wrapped around her hands provided her with unexpected comfort. For the first time since she arrived in Germany, she felt cared for, as though they were a patch of daffodils peeking out from beneath a layer of snow in spring's last snowstorm.

"We'll get all of your homework assignments for you, so don't you worry about that," Donna said.

"That's right, you just feel better," Sarah said. "I'm sure the teachers will understand, too."

By now, Gabrielle had opened her eyes and was looking up at her friends, but all she could do was give them half a smile.

"Okay, girls, let her rest now," the nurse said, gesturing toward the doorway.

"We're leaving," Donna said to the nurse, then turned back to Gabrielle, "We'll bring your homework over later."

As they were leaving, Essie walked in.

"See you later," Gabrielle said to her friends.

"She can go home," the nurse said to Essie.

"Do you know what caused it?" Essie asked.

"She fainted, so it could be anything. Dehydration is possible. Lack of enough to eat could have been the cause. Did she eat breakfast before leaving home this morning?"

"I don't know; she left before I saw her." Essie stood with her arms folded lightly across her stomach as she spoke to the nurse, barely acknowledging Gabrielle, who was still curled up on the table.

Finally, the nurse walked over to Gabrielle and removed the white blanket. Gabrielle stepped down from the table and left with Essie.

"Did you eat breakfast?" Essie asked as they walked down the school corridor.

"Yes." Gabrielle felt ashamed for lying, but she didn't want to tell Essie all she drank was half a glass of orange juice because she was in a hurry to leave before she or Edgar emerged from their bedroom.

"Well, get some rest at home," said Essie.

Not another word was spoken until they returned to the apartment, and Gabrielle said, "I'll be in my room."

Essie put the car keys down on the kitchen counter and turned on the television to her favorite soap opera before saying, "Dinner is at seven."

Gabrielle cringed, knowing Edgar would be home for dinner.

GABRIELLE OPENED HER journal and took the pen off the nightstand. The fog in her mind was starting to lift to the point where she began asking a lot of questions, almost all of which were directed at God. With her pen in hand, she wrote:

Dear God,

I'm sitting here in complete confusion, pain, and even isolation. Did you know that I fainted in class today because everything became too overwhelming? I need to know: where were you in my time of need? I saw your beauty in the lake's reflection. I saw your love in the whites of the clouds. I saw your promise in the blue of the sky. But, where were you in that dreadful moment?

Please send me the answers.

Love,

Gaby

Chapter Nine

"THE CRACKING OF a ruler on our desks never failed to startle me," Gabrielle explained as she peeled an orange. "The sound alone always sent quivers down each vertebra. I always felt sorry for the student who was the target of the nun's anger."

Donna took a sip from her chocolate milk before saying, "I can't imagine growing up going to Catholic school."

"Me neither," said Sarah. With her free hand, she brushed her long hair off her face and away from her sandwich.

They were sitting in the stairwell that led from the cafeteria to the outdoors a floor down. It was a spot they had discovered a few weeks earlier, and had made it their new escape from the other students. None of the teachers stopped them from going through the door to the stairway, or perhaps they hadn't even noticed. The girls could talk a little louder, and not feel as though all eyes were on them, or rather not on them at all. They could be themselves for a half-hour during their school day.

A fresh layer of snow had fallen that morning while they were in class, leaving a blanket of unscathed snow across the schoolyard. Later, when the bell would ring, crisscrossing footprints would render it tainted.

"Considering the school was all-girls, I was rather surprised that the ruler cracked as often as it did. There were no boys to create mischief the way they do here. If this were a Catholic school, we would be hearing the snap of a ruler every five minutes. No one would ever get any work done."

Sarah and Donna laughed in agreement. Gabrielle bit into her ham sandwich and licked a splattering of mustard from her finger. "By the time I was in middle school some of the girls had learned their lessons, but others were still subject to the wrath of the nuns." Gabrielle didn't need to mention that she had always been able to escape punishment. Donna and Sarah would know that about her.

"Are you giving anyone a Valentine, Gabrielle?" Sarah asked.

"I haven't thought much about it." When in fact Gabrielle had thought about it quite a bit.

The week earlier she had mailed Benji a Valentine card. It was no ordinary Valentine card because she had decided to pour her heart out in a poem for him. Seven months had passed since she boarded the plane to Germany. Only a few months had passed since Sasha told her Benji was seeing someone else. Still, Gabrielle continued to believe that despite all of those days, weeks, and months, she would eventually hear from her beloved Benji. In her heart, she knew they were meant for one another, and as far as she knew, the heart didn't lie.

But it did break. It could shatter into millions of pieces in an instant. Between missing Benji, and in order to cope with Edgar's betrayal—and feeling so utterly violated—she had written more poetry and journal entries than ever before. When she wrote to Benji, she now personally mailed the letters either on the way to or from school. She didn't want Edgar's hands touching the envelopes, nor did she want him knowing she was still mailing letters to her love in Haiti.

The Valentine poem she had written for Benji before school that morning nearly begged him for his now seemingly unrequited love. With a dabbing of perfume on the envelope, she walked the letter to the mailbox, gripping it between gloved fingers, and dropped it in the box with hopes that maybe it would be the one he would respond to.

Tell me

Tell me when you gaze into my eyes
You are drowned in my sea of love
Tell me my heart exudes
This exhilarating fragrance of love
That you inhale while thinking about me
Tell me, tell me without me
Your life is an empty and endless cave
Where you lose yourself aimlessly
Tell me, tell me my love
That your life is meaningless
Without me
Tell me that the sweet fragrance of my heart in love
Fills your heart with happiness
Tell me my darling
That on my lips you tasted
The sweet nectar of love
Tell me that with me you have
A reason to live
Tell me, prince of my heart
That you want to spend the rest of
Your days in the bosom of our love
Tell me, apple of my eye that
You'll love me until the end of your days
Promise me that you'll love me
Through eternity
Promise me that we will live only
For each other
Tell me, just tell me you love me

Sasha had indicated they were talking marriage, but Gabrielle would see visions of him ending it with this new woman, visions of telling her that Gabrielle was the only one he could ever spend the rest of his days with. She also knew that he had his reasons for not mailing her back, and she refused to make up excuses for him. All she could do was continue to love him, and so she did...in every moment of every day because that was what kept her going. It was what got her through the longest, coldest winter of her life.

Because of this, Gabrielle had determined that while Sasha would never lie to her, she would continue sending love letters to Benji until he personally told her to stop. She knew intuitively that he loved receiving them, and since he hadn't contacted her otherwise, and because it helped to keep her grounded, the letters continued. Her only concern was whether or not Edgar would notice the stamps missing from the large roll that he kept in a drawer in a table in the dining room. The drawer had envelopes, stamps, pens, and other necessities.

GABRIELLE'S FRIENDSHIP WITH Donna and Sarah had been her other salvation. She was too petrified to open up to them about what had happened with Edgar, mostly because that was something she also wanted to keep private while she sorted through her tumultuous emotions that ranged from shame to fear and more. She also didn't want them to present any feelings of them being uncomfortable around him. She wasn't sure anymore of what he was fully capable of, but she was relatively certain he wouldn't touch them.

It was rare that they came over to the apartment, and most times when they did he wasn't there. Essie seemed bothered by their presence, however, which was something Gabrielle could not figure out. Emmanuel, on the other hand, seemed to enjoy it when the two girls came around. For the most part, however, the three girls chose to study in the library after school and walked to and from school together.

Occasionally they went shopping at the PX, but, Gabrielle, and Donna and Sarah for that matter, had little financial resources to spend money shopping. Edgar was particularly stringent with money to the point where Gabrielle began to wonder if Essie wasn't on the right track with her albeit unethical shopping tendencies. In fact, it was that very afternoon when Gabrielle was tempted for the first time to try it on her own.

"DO YOU TWO want to go shopping later? I have to pick up a few things," asked Gabrielle.

"I can't. I promised my mother I would help her with a project at home," said Sarah.

"Me neither," Donna piped in. "I have to rewrite that paper for English if I want to bring my grade up."

"Okay," Gabrielle said. "Next time then."

When the school bell rang later that afternoon, Gabrielle walked over to the PX. She made her way to the aisle with the drugstore items, looking specifically for sanitary pads. She had run out the month before, and forgot to ask Essie to pick some up.

As she made her way up and down the aisle, she found the brand she liked and noted the price. Since Essie had been buying them for her, she hadn't realized how much they cost. She checked her wallet, but only had a fraction of what she needed to pay for them.

She then looked over at the cash register only to see that there was a long line and that the clerk was busy ringing everyone up. She then looked over each shoulder. When she saw it was clear, she tucked the box of pads in her purse. Her rationale was that if anyone said anything, she could drop her purse and run; whereas, if the contents were stashed in her clothing, the evidence would be harder to ditch.

Gabrielle hesitated. She wasn't quite sure if she should keep browsing or if she should make a dash for the door. For a moment, she felt paralyzed and indecisive. But, as though someone else took over, she picked up her pace and walked out the door, just as she had done several months ago when Essie stuffed her purse with the blouse. This time, she felt a different rush. She needed the pads. She didn't have the money. But, most of all, she simply didn't care. She was on Edgar's turf, and knew that if she got caught, and he found out, she would pay a different price. In that moment, it just didn't matter though.

WHEN GABRIELLE ARRIVED home, she took the box of pads out of her purse and put them in the bathroom. An immense pang of guilt hit her when she pulled the box from her purse. Had there only been seven commandments, she would have been all right, but the fact was, the eighth one was the one she had just broken. Even worse, she had done so intentionally. Suddenly she found herself fretting over the number of Hail Maries and Our Fathers she would endure in order to achieve any level of forgiveness. She also felt a sense of remorse and regret come over her for being so harsh toward Essie for the same behavior.

Gabrielle had a better understanding of the temptation, and could even see how addicting it could become. The act was just easy enough to pull off that saying, "Just one more time," was purely conceivable. Add to it the rush that came from the fear of getting caught. However, the fear of the wrath of Edgar if she had been caught was a far greater deterrent than any schoolhouse nun had ever been. She knew a nun's strike of a ruler would pale in comparison to his punishment. Gabrielle gathered that Essie was better prepared for that than she would ever be. In that exact moment, Gabrielle looked in the mirror and faced herself. Really faced herself, as she looked right in her own eyes and vowed to never steal again. Never. She fell to her knees to pray and sobbed uncontrollably.

NO ONE ELSE was home, so she pulled out her journal and sat on the couch in the living room with a glass of milk and a small plate of cookies.

I did something today that I vowed to never do again. I stole. It was only a box of sanitary pads, but it wasn't about them. Ever since the incident, I feel...I don't know...like screaming, but I can't. I can't say a word to anyone because I'm so ashamed by what happened. I wonder every day where God was in that moment, and stealing just felt like something...well...something I could just do. It was an impulse, and it was wrong. I'm sorry God, but you weren't there for me when I needed you, and I did what I did today because, well, I guess because I was hurt. Why did Edgar do what he did? Where was God?

GABRIELLE CLOSED BOTH her journal and her eyes for a moment to gather her emotions. She hadn't meant to write down what happened, or to name Edgar, but it all flowed through her pen uncontrollably.

She silenced her mind until all she could hear was the ticking of the clock. That was when she decided to continue writing about other things, such as how she only had a few more months left of school and of her goals and desires for college.

In an effort to keep focused on her future, Gabrielle remembered back to her earlier years of school, when the curriculum became more demanding with tougher classes, such as social studies, geography, world history, literature, religion, and civics, all of which prepared her for her future. While she thrived in those classes, most of the girls enjoyed their home economics class where they learned how to sew, and as they got older, they learned how to take care of their household, how to be good wives, and how to be good mothers. Gabrielle, on the other hand, had a bigger vision for her life. She didn't talk about it outwardly, but she knew deep down that she was going to go places and do things beyond what was taught in home economics. Her goal was to earn her degree in business so that she could be an independent and self-sufficient woman one day.

If there was one thing that being raised by her mother and living with Edgar and Essie had taught her, it was that she wanted to be financially independent as soon as she could. She watched as Edgar controlled all of the money and how Essie had to work creatively around what little bit of funds he allotted her. She had even documented an entire page in her journal several weeks ago about how she would never let that happen to her. She would be self-sustaining, and a business degree from college would help her do that. She knew she had the grades, now she needed to find the college and graduate from the school she was in.

About an hour after she first sat down on the couch, the door opened and Essie and Emmanuel came through it.

“You’re back!” Gabrielle managed a smile at them, then stood up and took her journal to her room where she tucked it in the nightstand drawer before going back out to the kitchen to help unload groceries and to prepare dinner.

THE NEXT MORNING, and two and three mornings after that, Gabrielle began to wonder why her period hadn’t started. Each time she sat down on the toilet, anticipation was followed by disappointment. There were a few times she thought she felt cramps, but they were either false alarms or perhaps something she had eaten. By the fourth day after her period was due, she became increasingly nervous. How could this be? Even though she knew how, she couldn't fathom the possibility of being pregnant.

Finally, on that Saturday morning, now five days late, she went to Essie.

"Essie?" Gabrielle called to her as she entered their bedroom. She rarely went in there, but Edgar was traveling and she knew Essie was in there folding clothes from the dryer.

"Yes, Gabrielle?" She didn't look up from her task.

"I'm...well...I have a problem."

"What is it?" Essie put the shirt she was folding back down in the laundry basket and looked, for the first time, up at Gabrielle.

"My period. It's...it's late."

"Oh. Well, you're young. Your body is still figuring things out. I'm sure you'll get it any day now."

"It is already almost a week late. I am never late," Gabrielle twisted her palms together behind her back. Her feet shook as she stood in the doorway. She forced herself to remain as calm as possible. "I think I should go to the doctor. You know, make sure everything's okay."

"The clinic is open first thing Monday morning. I'll make an appointment. Maybe you'll get it by then," Essie said rather nonchalantly.

Gabrielle was a little surprised Essie hadn't asked how or if she could possibly pregnant. Feeling relief from that and because she would be able to go the clinic on Monday, she thanked Essie and left the room.

THE REST OF the weekend dragged even though she had plans with Donna and Sarah to make jewelry at Sarah's, whose parents were away for the weekend. They had the apartment to themselves for a slumber party on Saturday night, and Gabrielle was only able to go because Edgar was traveling and Essie went out on a limb and said it was okay. Partly because Sarah's apartment was only a few floors down in the same building, and also because Essie's sister, Stella, had expectantly arrived from out of town. Essie set her up in the extra bed in Gabrielle's room. By Gabrielle not being there for a night, Stella had some privacy.

Gabrielle was in her bedroom packing for Sarah's when Essie said, "My sister Stella is flying in tonight, so you'll get to see her tomorrow when you come home. She remembers you fondly from her visit to see Edgar a few years ago in Haiti, so I'm sure the two of you will do just fine in here."

Essie made her way to the other bed so she could put clean sheets on the bed for Stella.

"Oh, is everything okay with her?" Gabrielle asked while she packed an overnight bag before diligently making room in her closet and dresser, pleasing Essie. Her heart sank with the news. Now more than ever she needed her space to sort through the aftermath of losing her innocence, of losing faith in family, and even in God. But, there were still several months left of school before she could leave that summer, and every day of being under the same roof as Edgar was a struggle.

Facing Essie was also very difficult. Did she even realize just what Edgar was capable of?

"She's going through some, well, personal things, so we said she could come here for a bit," said Essie. "You know how it is to want to escape."

Gabrielle was not sure if that last comment was meant to be as genuine as Essie made it sound. Even still, Gabrielle remembered meeting Stella when she came to visit Edgar at their father's house in Haiti. Edgar had stayed with his and Gabrielle's father during his trips to Haiti. Their father lived an opulent lifestyle with a lush yard and large pool. That was the day when they had been able to get to know one another, and went out for ice cream and swimming in the pool. It was also the day when Stella told Gabrielle that Emmanuel wasn't Essie's son.

The same age as Gabrielle, Stella was younger than Essie and was coming to stay with them so she could get her footing back after leaving a bad relationship.

"The two of you should be just fine in here. She can settle in while you are at your friend's tonight," said Essie. She never did call Sarah and Donna by their names, for reasons Gabrielle never understood.

Even after hearing more from Essie about Stella's reason for her stay, Gabrielle still had mixed emotions. On the one hand, she liked Stella and was looking forward to the company. On the other hand, she not only craved her privacy, but having been raised as an only child, she never had to share a bedroom before. However, Gabrielle vowed to make the most of it, despite the inner turmoil she was struggling with.

Gabrielle put one last T-shirt in her bag and zipped it up.

"I'm leaving now," she said to Essie as she left the bedroom. After closing the apartment door, she stepped into the elevator, pressing the button for Sarah's floor. She loved the rush an elevator gave.

"Let's bake some chocolate chip cookies!" Donna said as she wrapped up making a necklace from colorful beads and a thin string of leather. She held the necklace up and observed it before hooking it around her neck.

"I have to check the kitchen to see if we have all the ingredients," Sarah said. "Let's go look."

The three made their way from the living room where strings and beads and plastic boxes had taken over the floor.

"The chocolate chips should be in here," Sarah said as she reached up high in one of the cabinets. "Gabrielle, can you get the eggs and milk from the fridge?"

"Sure," Gabrielle said. As she walked toward the refrigerator, she felt a pang and clutched her stomach.

"Are you okay?" Donna asked.

"Yeah, I think so." Gabrielle hoped they were cramps starting and stood up tall to stretch her arms over her head in hopes they would work their way out. The pang ceased as she stretched, and she went back to pulling the dairy items from the refrigerator. However, while Donna and Sarah mixed the ingredients, Gabrielle excused herself. Once in the bathroom, she broke down in tears when she realized her period still had not arrived.

A knock came on the door and Gabrielle heard Donna and Sarah.

"Gabrielle, are you okay?" they asked in unison.

"I will be," she said. She was leaning against the sink and reached over and opened the door. The two girls on the other side were clearly shaken by how upset Gabrielle was.

"No, you're not okay! What's going on? You can tell us anything, you know that," Donna said.

"Yes, anything. What is it?" asked Sarah. She reached for a box of tissues and handed one to Gabrielle.

"My period," cried Gabrielle. She wasn't sure what else to say about it or how wide she wanted to open the door of information.

"What about it? You got it? I have pads, don't worry," said Sarah.

"No, that's not it. I didn't get it. I'm late...several days late," Gabrielle said and started crying again.

Donna and Sarah put their arms around Gabrielle and waited until the tears subsided and her breathing calmed down again.

"Well, I'm sure it's just something silly. Bodies can be weird and you've been through a lot with the move here, a new school, living with family you weren't used to living with. It's a lot for anyone to go through," said Donna.

For the moment, Gabrielle felt better and decided to keep her secret. After all, Donna could be right. She had been through a lot.

They made their way out of the bathroom and back into the kitchen where the timer was just about to go off. When Sarah put on a mitt and opened the oven door, a waft of warm air with the scrumptious smell of chocolate chip cookies made its way to the girls' faces, which were all smiling.

I

"YOUR APPOINTMENT IS at eight thirty. I'll take you to school afterwards," Essie said.

She had knocked on Gabrielle's door at seven, several minutes before her alarm would go off.

"Okay, thanks," said Gabrielle.

Essie left, closing the door behind her and Gabrielle rolled out of her bed. Stella lay asleep in her bed facing the wall and away from Gabrielle, who hadn't arrived home from Sarah's until late Sunday afternoon. The family had been playing cards in the living room and roped her into playing a few rounds. They were up later than usual for a Sunday, and Gabrielle gathered it was because Stella was there that Edgar made the exception.

The doctor's appointment allowed Gabrielle a bit of extra time that morning. While Stella remained asleep in the bed across the room, Gabrielle reached into her nightstand drawer and pulled out her journal. Immediately, she knew something was off. The loose papers that had been stuck between certain pages were now shoved in the back and were in no particular order.

She turned the journal over as though it would have answers to what happened to it on the back. It naturally didn't, and she turned it back over and started flipping through the pages. It only took a moment before she realized that someone had been reading it. The question was, who? Stella? Essie? Emmanuel? Edgar? Her face turned red with the heat of anger rising from her heart to her throat. How could they? Her first inclination was Stella, but she had learned long ago not to make poor assumptions. She thought back to the night before when they were all playing cards. No one seemed out of sorts with her, as she might have expected if they had invaded her privacy and now knew her deepest secrets.

Gabrielle put her journal on her lap and unwillingly absorbed the betrayal. She had once heard that betrayal was God's way of showing you who you needed to cut ties with, but she felt like she had no escape, that she was trapped. Trapped in a home where she had been betrayed in so many unexpected ways. Trapped in the feeling that Benji had let her go, but in not being able to accept that truth. And now her personal life was trapped in the mind of a relative, only she had not a clue which one.

It was then when it dawned on her that it could have been more than one. Suddenly the vision of Essie and Stella turning pages, pointing at what Gabrielle had written, and giggles erupting between them flashed before her. With that thought, she ran to the bathroom and threw up.

The long, hot shower calmed Gabrielle down to the point where she was able to ready herself for the doctor's appointment. When she came out of her bedroom dressed and ready to go, she found Essie and Stella in the living room. Essie had her purse in hand, seemingly ready to go, while Stella sat on the couch with a cup of coffee. Gabrielle couldn't look either one of them in the eye, so she simply said, "I'm ready to go when you are."

"I'll be back after I drop her to school," Essie said to Stella.

Gabrielle was relieved to hear that Stella wasn't going with them. She really hadn't had much interaction with Stella since she arrived because Gabrielle had spent the weekend with her friends. Gabrielle found the two sisters to be quite similar in appearance, only Stella was a younger version of her sister.

When Gabrielle and Essie arrived at the clinic, the receptionist told her to take a seat and that the doctor would be with her soon. What seemed like three hours later was really only twelve minutes before the door opened and her name was called. The nurse was holding a chart as she watched Gabrielle walked toward her.

"How are you this morning?" the nurse asked.

"I can't really say I know the answer to that question yet," Gabrielle said. She half smirked, trying to find humor in the moment.

"What brings you in today?" the nurse asked once they were in an examination room.

"My period is nearly a week late. I'm never late." Gabrielle looked up at the nurse, hoping for an obvious and simple explanation. But her hope dwindled when she saw the look on the nurse's face.

"Have you had sexual intercourse since your last period?" The nurse asked almost too matter-of-factly.

Gabrielle paused for a moment, not knowing how to answer. Clearly if the test results come back that she's pregnant she would be lying if she said no. At the same time, she didn't know how much further the nurse was going to press her for information. She was not ready to discuss what had happened that day with anyone. Nor did she know what the ramifications would be if people found out what Edgar had done. Would Edgar be discharged from the army? Would they tell Essie, who sat in the waiting room, what her husband had done?

Unable to actually speak, but wanting to answer the nurse, she reluctantly nodded her head yes.

The next thing she knew, the nurse was handing her a tiny plastic cup with a label on it. "We need a urine sample."

"For what?" asked Gabrielle.

"A pregnancy test," the nurse responded in an almost curt tone.

Feeling ashamed, Gabrielle took the cup and went into the bathroom. When she emerged, the nurse left the room with the sample and said she'd be back with the results.

While waiting, Gabrielle wondered if they were always so casual with patients or if it was just with potentially pregnant teenagers that they leaned toward being curt. She imagined if it had been Essie sitting there in the gown, the two would be chatting about how she would tell her husband she was pregnant and guessing whether it was a boy or a girl.

The door opened again and this time a tall, male phlebotomist came in with the nurse. He asked her to sit still while he wrapped an elastic band around her arm to draw blood.

"The urine test came back positive, but because of your age, we need to do a blood test to make extra sure," explained the nurse.

Gabrielle winced as the needle went in, and nearly fainted by the reality of being pregnant and the drawing of her blood. She needed all she could to keep from passing out!

Convincing herself to settle down, and in an odd way, she felt that perhaps the drawing of the blood would draw the experience itself out of her. She knew this wouldn't be a reality, but she played with the fantasy in the moments that the phlebotomist held the small glass tube that slowly filled.

"We will call you later today with the final results," the nurse said after the phlebotomist left.

"Thank you," Gabrielle said. Final results? The urine test could be wrong? She only hoped.

LATER, IN SCHOOL, the only thing Gabrielle seemed to be able to accomplish was watching the ticking hands on the clock. When she walked in the door to the apartment later that afternoon, the look on Essie's face told her what she needed to know. It was what she had been dreading all week.

"You're pregnant..."

"Is that what the clinic said?" Gabrielle was hoping that she might have a moment of still questioning before the reality gripped her.

"How did this happen? Who is he?" Essie asked.

"I don't know!" Gabrielle screamed.

"How can you not know?"

"I just don't! I don't know what else to say." Gabrielle's voice turned soft with that last sentence. The truth was, she really had no idea what to tell Essie. She didn't have any idea what to do next. So, she did what she always did—she went to her room and wrote in her journal. She could hear Essie saying something to her as she walked down the hallway, but none of the words registered.

New
Farewell innocence
Farewell carefree life
Farewell free spirit
Farewell dreams of love
Farewell fairytale ending
New life
New challenge
New uncertainty
New despair
New sigh
New future
New tears
New deceptions
What to do?

The hardest part of the whole situation that Gabrielle had yet to be able to accept, nor would she ever be able to, was that she had promised herself that the gift of her virginity would someday belong to Benji. She so often thought about their love transpiring through that moment and how that night would be...she knew they would be married, and most of all that their lovemaking would be out of mutual love. To that extent, she had even fantasized that they would conceive their first baby. In only a few short moments, Edgar had stripped her of that dream, and so much more.

She turned the page and wrote to God:

It is the complete unfairness that I can't understand, God. Edgar's words that I "owed him that" echo in my head late at night when I lay in bed. Those moments late at night had always been reserved for my dreams of Benji, and now they are destroyed by the reality of Edgar. The reality that my life is no longer what I knew it to be. And now...now there is a child. My child. His child. Not mine and Benji's. Why, God? Why?

Chapter Ten

Wednesday night when Edgar came home, Emmanuel and Gabrielle were both in the living room doing homework. He came through the door in his usual gruff manner, putting his bags down right inside, knowing that Essie would gather them later.

"Who's home?" asked Edgar. The minute the sound of his voice filled the apartment, Gabrielle felt the tension fill the room.

"We are!" said Emmanuel. He held up his homework to show his father he was being good.

"Good to see," said Edgar. "Where's your mother?"

"I think she's in your room," said Gabrielle. She looked closely at Edgar's face, trying to get a read as to whether or not he knew she was pregnant. At the same time, looking at his face made her stomach turn. She didn't know if Essie had told him anything. Usually when he traveled they didn't talk very often. If he was gone for only a few days, they rarely talked at all.

So Gabrielle gathered that he didn't know yet, but if he did, she wanted to get a sense of it first. Gabrielle told Essie that Edgar would have to hear from Gabrielle herself that she was pregnant. She knew she would rather do it than have him hear it from Essie. Besides, had Essie told him, Gabrielle wasn't sure where that conversation would lead. She knew deep down that she had to be the one to tell him. But it was still the most dreaded conversation of her life. Worse, even, than telling Benji she was moving to Germany.

"Essie!" Edgar called down the hall. "I'm home!"

"I'm right here," Essie said as she made her way from their bedroom. "We already ate, but there's a warm plate for you in the oven. It's meatloaf."

Edgar went to the kitchen to pull the plate out of the oven with a pair of hot mitts while Essie picked up his luggage and headed toward the laundry room. From experience, she knew that most of it was going to go in the washing machine right away. Once the washing machine was running, she took the luggage and the rest of its contents to their bedroom. Edgar sat down at the dining room table with Gabrielle and Emmanuel to eat his dinner. The only sound for a while was from his silverware hitting the plate and the turning of the pages from the newspaper that he was reading. Emmanuel finished his homework and began reading a book while Gabrielle worked on her American History paper. Eventually, the quiet room made her too nervous and she put away her books and notebook. She glanced at Edgar to see that he was contently eating. She knew she didn't want to talk to him that night and would likely wait a few more days until the weekend.

After putting her books in her room, Gabrielle went into the bathroom. The day before she had spotted the box of sanitary pads in the cabinet under the sink, thinking how they weren't worth stealing after all. She knew that throwing them out would be wasteful, and would only raise questions if anyone saw them in the garbage can. Yet, her instinct had been to throw them against the wall, letting the shattered cardboard box explode as she watched the sanitary pads float down to the ground like large snowflakes in a late winter storm. She was certain the visual wasn't as satisfactory as actually doing it, but she had always been one to curtail her anger and rarely had outbursts. Crying and feeling frustration went hand-in-hand, but rarely did she act out, only adding negative behavior.

Her strongest sense of frustration came from the reality that Edgar had been the one to impregnate her, secondary was hearing the news from Essie. At seventeen years old, these were not the kinds of frustrations she thought she would bear. She had come to Germany for an education that would lead her to the college of her choice and a better life, not a situation that would make her have to choose life itself. Her Catholic upbringing taught her that abortion was not an option. At the same time, she had no resources to raise a child, a child born from sin. The child she hadn't planned for, let alone under the circumstances.

No, these were not the kinds of frustrations she had expected to face at seventeen. Final exams, term papers, meeting new friends, and cold weather were really all she had planned for when the nose of the plane touched ground in Germany.

For the meantime, the box of sanitary pads remained stored away under the sink until some day when she would need them again. She thought about how by the time that day would come, she would have given birth to a child. It was that thought that made the room start to spin. Afraid she might faint again, she went back into her bedroom and settled in for the night. She was just about to turn out the light when Stella came in the room.

"Oh, good. You're still awake," said Stella as she quietly closed the door behind her.

"Yes, but just barely. Everything okay?" asked Gabrielle.

"Sure, yes. Except there's something I need to ask you. To talk to you about. Can you stay awake for a few more minutes?"

Gabrielle couldn't imagine what Stella wanted to talk to her about. Her first expectation was to hear a confession that Stella had read Gabrielle's journal. So, she was surprised when Stella started talking again.

"It's Essie. I'm worried about her, so I thought maybe you could fill me in a bit since you've been here a while now."

Gabrielle sat up in her bed and hugged her pillow to her stomach. "Like what?" On some level she was relieved that they weren't discussing the contents of her journal, but at the same time she tread lightly.

"Well, Essie seems different. Like she holding a lot in."

"What do you mean? Emotionally?" *Join the club!*

"Well yes, but I guess it has to do more with when Edgar is around. I noticed that she becomes, oh, what would you call it? Reserved, maybe? Like she walks on eggshells around him. When he's not here, I see glimpses of the Essie I know, but when he's here it's very different. I haven't seen her quite like this before."

Stella climbed in her bed, having changed into her nightgown. "So, I wondered if you noticed the same behavior?"

Gabrielle thought for a moment, not quite ready to answer. When she did, she lowered her voice and said, "I think you are right to a point. Emmanuel is a good kid, but he can be a handful, too, and Edgar expects perfection in everything. The kitchen has to be clean, the rugs vacuumed, you know what I mean. The house is spotless because that is how he demands it to be every minute. At the same time, Essie knew she was marrying a military man. That's often how they are. It's in their blood, their training. Does that make sense?"

Gabrielle wasn't sure where all of that logic came from, and she knew it wasn't enough to satisfy Stella, but at the same time, it kept her answer away from the emotional ramifications that Stella first alluded to.

"I just left a bad relationship, so I suppose I'm more sensitive to it, but I just wish Essie had more of her own life to live for. It seems to be all about Edgar. His schedule, his needs, his child, his everything." Stella fluffed her bed and lay down with her arms folded behind her head.

"I know what you mean," said Gabrielle, knowing full well that Stella had no idea how well she knew.

"Thanks for listening. I'll try to talk to Essie before I leave. Goodnight," said Stella.

"Goodnight." Gabrielle turned off the light and fluffed her own pillow.

I

BY THE TIME the weekend came, Gabrielle had gone through a roller coaster of emotions about telling Edgar of her pregnancy. She had phrased and rephrased the conversation dozens of times in her mind, never finding the right words. She knew he was leaving again on Monday for a short trip and had decided that telling him on Sunday night would be her best move. With him leaving the next day, and the weekend mostly behind them, that would leave little time for them to have to interact once he knew.

"I received notice from the school that your volleyball team will be traveling this spring. You need to get a physical in order to be able to go," Edgar told Gabrielle on Saturday night during dinner. Stella and Emmanuel paid no attention to the conversation, but Essie looked up from her plate and directly at Gabrielle. She knew Gabrielle had not told him yet because the apartment had been too peaceful, nor had he come to her about it. "Schedule an appointment at the clinic this week so you can go with your team."

"Yes, sir." Gabrielle wasn't sure what else to say. She knew that he would be furious if he later found out that she already knew of her pregnancy and didn't tell him, but agreed to go for the physical.

Gabrielle had already been worried about what to do regarding the traveling volleyball team. Sarah and Donna had begged her to go to tryouts with them several weeks earlier, Gabrielle welcomed the opportunity to play again since she really enjoyed the game. She was the captain of her volleyball team in Haiti and was actually good at it. Her height certainly gave her an advantage over the other girls. The coach took extra time to work with her to hone her skills around the extra several inches advantage she carried.

When she found out she was pregnant, that was one of the many things that swam around in her head, knowing that she would be disappointing everyone by not being able to go on the trip. She knew the physical was a requirement because several of the girls had already gone for theirs. The coach had asked her if she had gone in yet, and Gabrielle used the excuse that Edgar was traveling and was unable to sign off on the papers just yet.

She felt horrible about keeping the truth from everyone, and somehow managed to rise above pitying herself. At the very least, she hoped to be able to travel with them, if anything to get away for a bit, even if she couldn't play. She was certain she could serve the team in some way off the court. The trick was juggling the timing of all of the balls in the air that were coming down on her at once.

When Sunday evening came, Gabrielle asked Essie to keep Emmanuel and Stella busy while she spoke to Edgar. Essie agreed, naturally, and took them out after dinner. Amazingly, Edgar didn't ask where they were going when Essie told him they had an errand to run. Gabrielle noticed that he seemed to ask fewer questions of Essie's whereabouts ever since Stella's arrival.

Gabrielle was in the bathroom washing her face when she heard the apartment door close. She knew her window of opportunity had just opened and that she had no choice but to take it.

When she peeked out the door, she saw that Edgar was sitting on the couch reading the paper. Somehow she found the courage to put one foot in front of the other, which lead her down the hall, in order to talk to him.

She pulled out a chair and took a seat at the dining room table, purposely putting the table between where he was sitting and herself. She stared at the wall over his shoulder for a moment until he put the newspaper down and looked up at her.

"What's going on?" he asked.

Gabrielle took a deep breath. Here it goes.

"I, uh, won't be able to go on the trip with the volleyball team after all." Gabrielle's eyes began to swell with tears. She gripped tightly to the seat of the chair she was sitting in.

"Why is that?" Edgar asked.

"Because...I'm pregnant."

If silence can really be deafening, it was proven in that moment. Gabrielle waited for what seemed like forever for any kind of flinch or scream or reaction from Edgar. Instead, they sat there in a silent stare-off. The familiar ticking of the clock on the wall above even faded to silence. However, when the reality struck Edgar, it was like a bolt of lightning, and he was off the couch in a flash slamming his hands down on the dining room table screaming at her.

"This is all your fault!" he spat. He then began pacing back and forth across the dining room floor. His hands were on his head, gripping his scalp and pulling at his own hair. Gabrielle didn't dare say a word. "Are you sure? You've been tested?"

Gabrielle nodded yes, never looking up from the table. Her eyes had locked on the candlestick in front of her.

"Does Essie know about this?" Suddenly, Edgar's anger reached another level.

Gabrielle nodded yes again.

"Say something!" demanded Edgar.

With that, Gabrielle opened up and the words began spewing out. "Yes, she knows! She took me to the clinic last week. And, this is not my fault! It's not my fault at all! My whole life is ruined because of you!" Gabrielle pointed directly at Edgar. "I had plans. I was going to go to college. And now, what? What am I supposed to do with a baby? A baby! What you decide to tell Essie is up to you! I already have enough of my own life to figure out!"

Gabrielle shocked not only herself, but also Edgar with her outburst. The same instinct of flight or fight came to mind, but once again, she knew that flight wasn't an option. She had to confront him, to stand up to him. Even more so, she had to let some of the pent up emotions out. It had been building inside for weeks, and though her boiling point was higher than most, it had been reached.

"Really? Your life?" Edgar swung his arms in the air. "Think about it, Gaby. This is really an easy fix; you go get an abortion. That's it. You can have your so-called life back, and the situation is solved," said Edgar.

Gabrielle detected a hint of trembling in his voice. He had stopped pacing and stood at the other end of the dining room table. His hands stopped flaring and were now planted on the back of a chair. Gabrielle was certain he would crush it if he applied any more pressure, she just wasn't sure if he was more afraid or angry in that moment. He had to be afraid that Essie would find out what he had done. And even though he was, for all intents and purposes, the head of the household, he had to have some level of shame for what he did. Gabrielle couldn't imagine that he would want Essie to find out the truth. It was Gabrielle's only leverage—her only saving grace in this situation.

"You know I was raised Catholic; an abortion is not an option. I don't know what the answer is, but I will tell you this..." Gabrielle was shaking, but somewhere from within she found the power to continue. "As God is my witness, you will pay for this!"

Edgar slammed his fist down on the table. Everything rattled. The candlesticks fell over. "You ungrateful brat! I bring you into my home and give you a whole new life—and this is what you do?"

"Yes, you gave me a whole new life! Just not the life I wanted, including that of an innocent child to bear!"

It was when those words were spewed across the table that the front door opened and Essie, Stella, and Emmanuel came through it. Gabrielle turned and ran out the door, brushing by the three of them. She didn't stop running until she reached the elevator, and after pushing the down button once, she had not the patience to stay and wait for it; she turned and ran the extra distance to the stairwell. Jumping down each flight until she reached the ground level, she burst out the main door for the apartment building and into the cold air of the night.

Gabrielle inhaled deeply. She watched closely as she exhaled; her breath was illuminated by the streetlight overhead.

"Gabrielle? Are you okay?" A voice in the shadows called out.

Gabrielle swung around in the direction of the voice to see Sarah walking down the sidewalk with a bag of groceries in her hands.

At the sight of her friend, Gabrielle burst into tears and put her head in her hands. She kept shaking her head no.

"What is it? What happened?" Sarah placed the groceries down on the wall and put her arm around Gabrielle, letting her cry.

Gabrielle's stomach started hurting from crying and breathing in cold air at the same time. With a few gasps, she eventually stopped and took a solid, deep breath. Finally, she was able to look over at Sarah, who sat there waiting patiently for any sign of what was wrong.

"I won't be able to travel with the volleyball team...," Gabriel started.

"That's what has you so upset?"

"No, it's the reason why." Gabrielle paused, torn as to whether or not to tell her friend. At the same time, she needed someone to talk to. "I'm pregnant," she finally said. Gabrielle watched closely to see Sarah's reaction.

"Oh no," said Sarah. "I don't know what to say. I can tell you're not okay, though. Anything you need or want to tell me, I'm here for you." Deep down, Gabrielle wondered if Sarah would understand the situation.

Sarah gave Gabrielle a hug. "It's cold out and you don't have a jacket on, Gabrielle. Let's go inside. If you need to come over to talk to my mom, if you think she can help, I'm sure she would listen or have some advice."

"Thank you, but probably not tonight. I don't know what I'm going to do yet." Gabrielle shivered as they approached the front door and entered through it. This time, she took the elevator. When they landed on Sarah's floor, Sarah assured Gabrielle that everything would be okay and told her she knew where to find her if she needed her.

"Thank you. I'll see you in the morning," said Gabrielle.

Gabrielle was shocked by what she saw when she walked through her apartment door. Plates, books, cloth napkins from their holders on the table, and even the candlesticks were strewn about the living room floor. She could hear Edgar and Essie screaming in their bedroom. It didn't take but a second for her to turn around and run back to the elevator. Once inside, she pushed the button for the fifth floor, and when the door opened again, she found herself knocking on Sarah's door. When Sarah and her mother opened the door, they found Gabrielle standing there shaking and crying. Sarah's mother grabbed a blanket from the linen closet and wrapped it around Gabrielle. Sarah's father sat at the kitchen table, and smiled warmly at Gabrielle. Sarah made two cups of hot chocolate.

In a short amount of time, Gabrielle was sitting on the couch wrapped in a blanket sipping hot chocolate, and for the first time in her almost eighteen years of life, she felt what true family was like. She wished she could bask in it for a long, long time.

Gabrielle overheard Sarah's mother on the phone with Essie, telling her that Gabrielle would be sleeping at their place that night.

"Do you need to talk," Sarah's mother asked when she hung up the phone. "We can go in Sarah's room, if you'd like."

"Perhaps. I don't know what to do or say, though. It's, well...complicated," said Gabrielle. She took another sip of her hot chocolate and adjusted the blanket across her legs.

"Anything you say would be between us. Just let me know if you want to talk, okay?"

"Yes, ma'am. Thank you," Gabrielle smiled at Sarah's mother.

"Let's go back to my room anyway. I still have some homework to finish and you can relax. I have spare pajamas you can borrow." Sarah stood up from the couch and Gabrielle followed, towing the blanket behind her.

Gabrielle changed into the pajamas Sarah gave her while Sarah sat at her desk finishing her last few math problems. Eventually she closed her math book and turned to face Gabrielle.

"I'm worried about you. I can't imagine being pregnant, but do you want to talk about it?" she asked.

Gabrielle sat on the guest bed against the far wall. She looked away from Sarah, hoping to be able to stare out the window into the dark, but the blinds were already drawn.

Right then Sarah's mother knocked on the door.

"Come in," Sarah called.

"I just wanted to say goodnight," her mother said as she stepped into the room.

"Do you want her to stay?" asked Sarah.

Gabrielle nodded yes, and picked up the pillow so she could hug it tight to her chest, to ground her. Sarah's mother closed the door behind her and pulled up a chair next to Gabrielle's bed. "You can tell us anything, Gabrielle."

Gabrielle looked over at Sarah who nodded her head, indicating to Gabrielle that she could tell her mom.

"I already told Sarah earlier tonight. She found me outside crying and I thought...well, I thought I could go back home, but I couldn't. It was ugly up there." Gabrielle looked down at her hands.

"What is it, dear? What did you tell Sarah?"

"That...umm...that I'm pregnant."

Sarah's mom turned her head and looked at Sarah before turning back to Gabrielle, who finally looked up at her. She welcomed the look of concern she found in her eyes, grateful to have a mother figure who might know what to do, or who could at least offer some sort of compassion.

"Does your family know?" she asked.

"Yes, I told Edgar tonight. Essie already knew. That's why it's kind of crazy up there right now." Gabrielle thought back to the scene in the living room that she left behind a few hours ago. "I needed somewhere to go, so thank you for letting me stay here tonight. It's just one night, I promise."

"It's no burden whatsoever," Sarah's mother assured Gabrielle. "So, you have gone to the clinic and have been tested?"

"Yes, both urine and blood said I was. Isn't this just great? Seventeen and a baby on the way."

"Have you decided to keep it?" Sarah's mother asked.

"Yes, my Catholic upbringing...well, you know, abortions are not the solution," said Gabrielle. "I just don't know yet what I'm going to do about the whole situation. All Sarah and I talk about are what colleges we want to go to, things like that. Not about babies. Not now. Not yet, anyway."

"I understand. Right now, I think the best thing for you is to get some rest. We are always here for you, so you be sure to feel comfortable coming to talk to us, okay?"

"Yes, ma'am. Thank you again for everything," Gabrielle lay down on the bed as Sarah's mother stood and returned the chair to its corner spot. Sarah had already changed into her pajamas and climbed into bed.

"Goodnight, girls." The door closed quietly as Sarah's mother left the room.

"You're lucky to have such a great mom," said Gabrielle.

"I thought she would at least be a good listener for you," said Sarah. She turned the light off on the nightstand. "Will you be okay to go to school tomorrow?"

"Yes, I'll go upstairs and change early enough to meet you."

"Good," said Sarah.

Gabrielle took a breath and said, "Sarah?"

"Yes?"

"It was Edgar. He did this."

The room went silent again until Sarah finally said, "Oh my gosh!" Sarah rolled over in bed and propped herself up on her elbow to face Gabrielle, even if it was dark. "I wondered who it might have been, but Edgar?

Don't you worry, though, everything is going to be okay, Gabrielle."

"I hope you are right," said Gabrielle.

"It has to be," said Sarah as she lay back down.

Gabrielle felt some relief in letting her dark secret out into the light, albeit a dim light.

They lay in silence until only their breaths of sleep filled the room.

I

GABRIELLE WAS SLIGHTLY disoriented when she awoke the next morning in Sarah's room. Even though she had spent the night at Sarah's before, the emotions of the previous night had fogged her mind as she opened her eyes and looked around. Gabrielle climbed out of bed and went over to Sarah, who was just beginning to stir.

"I need to go up to my place to change and grab my backpack. I'll meet you outside, usual time."

"Are you doing okay?" asked Sarah.

"I think so. Haven't woken up enough to think about it," said Gabrielle. She smiled at Sarah and thanked her again.

Once she was dressed and put her shoes on, she slipped out of their apartment and took the elevator back up to her floor.

The door was unlocked when she went to open it. Essie must have unlocked it for her. She tiptoed down the hallway to the bathroom and showered.

After getting dressed and brushing her hair, there was a knock at the door. Edgar didn't wait for a response before opening it; he never did. He stuck his head in.

"I'll be back on Wednesday. Take care of it before I return." Not waiting for a response, he closed the door behind him.

Stella rolled over in her bed and asked, "What did Edgar want?"

"Nothing," said Gabrielle. "Go back to sleep if you want, it's still early."

Gabrielle didn't know whether or not Essie shared the news of pregnancy with Stella. Yes, they were sisters, but Gabrielle didn't get the sense that they shared everything.

During breakfast, and without giving too much away for Emmanuel to understand, Gabrielle said to Essie, "He doesn't have a say in this. God does, and God wants...well, you know what God wants."

Gabrielle didn't know how to filter the words to tell Essie that she was going to go through with the pregnancy. She had had enough time to think things through and decided her only option was to put the baby up for adoption. Perhaps it could have a good life with good parents. She knew that for both her, and the baby, it was the right solution.

Essie nodded her head, almost as though she welcomed the friction between Gabrielle and Edgar.

WEDNESDAY NIGHT CAME all too quickly for Gabrielle. She knew the first thing Edgar would ask when he walked through the door was whether or not she had "taken care of it." She also knew that hiding in her bedroom wouldn't help, either. Instead, she brought her homework out into the living room and sat on the couch.

Emmanuel had taken up the entire dining room table with his project. There was paper, scissors, glue, and wooden sticks. He made his way around the table to different corners cutting and gluing, focused intently on his project.

Gabrielle was reading a chapter in her American History textbook when the front door opened and the all too familiar piece of luggage came through it first. It was set in the same place it always was, waiting for Essie to retrieve it. Next came the footsteps belonging to Edgar. Her body tightened up, instinctively preparing herself for the confrontation to come.

"I'm home!" Edgar yelled down the hall to Essie. He then looked over at Emmanuel and Gabrielle. Gabrielle didn't look up from her book, and Emmanuel quickly started telling him the intricate details of his project. Edgar feigned paying attention, but he was more intent on looking at Gabrielle for an answer. Feeling the weight of his stare, she finally looked up from her book and stared back at him with defiant eyes. That was all it took.

Edgar shook his head and retreated to the bedroom, leaving Gabrielle surprised and almost afraid of what could still come when he came back out. Like always though, Essie had left him a warm plate in the oven and when he returned, that was what he went for. By nine o'clock, he told Emmanuel it was his bedtime.

"Yes, sir," said Emmanuel. He cleaned up his project, said goodnight and left the room. When they were the only two left, Gabrielle was shocked by what came next.

Edgar put his fork down, looked up from his now empty plate, and said, “You have a sister.”

A sister? Gabrielle stared at him in disbelief, wondering where this conversation would go next and above all, who her sister is.

“What do you mean I have a sister?”

“She lives in Florida. Her name is Corinne.”

“Why didn’t I know about her? Why are you telling me now...” Gabrielle paused after that statement, and suddenly realized exactly why he was telling her now.

“I want you to call her and talk to her about the...pregnancy.” Edgar could barely speak the word, nor could he look at Gabrielle. “Her number is on the kitchen counter. If you call her in the morning before school, it will be afternoon her time. She’s expecting your call. You should go to her. She can help you in ways I...just accept her help.”

With that, Edgar stood and went to bed, leaving Gabrielle sitting in shock.

Chapter Eleven

CORINNE ANSWERED THE telephone on the first ring.

"Hello?"

"Corinne? This is Gaby. Gabrielle Namid. Um, I'm your sister." Gabrielle had been both nervous and excited about calling Corinne. "Is this a good time to call?" Edgar only had one picture of Corinne that he left next to the piece of paper with Corinne's phone number on it. It was taken several years ago; however, Gabrielle could see the family resemblance and felt an instant connection to the sister she never knew about.

"Of course! I'm so glad to hear your voice. Edgar filled me in a little bit on what has been going on, but why don't you tell me yourself." Her voice was very sympathetic and compassionate, and Gabrielle immediately felt comfortable talking to her.

"Well, I don't quite know where to start. But what I can tell you is that I came to Germany for my last year of school before going to college," Gabrielle took a deep breath, "and I just...I don't know if Edgar told you...but I just found out I am pregnant. It was completely unexpected. I have no idea what to do about it. Edgar is angry. Essie knows but hasn't asked any questions yet. One of my friends knows, and in a few months I guess everybody will know."

It was those last words that caused Gabrielle to choke up. She had only thought about her immediate surroundings regarding the pregnancy, and had not quite begun to look at it on a larger scale. Although she had thought about it in regards to her volleyball team, she had yet to put much thought into what everyone else would think. Starting with her classmates, her teachers, other people on the base, and even her friends and family back in Haiti. Of all of them, she had put most of her thought on Benji. Even when it came to him, there was only so much she would let herself think about. She had become quite good at closing down her mind, only allowing in possible solutions and scenarios, none of which were promising, but it had been her survival tool.

"I'm so sorry, Gaby. No seventeen-year-old should have to be making these decisions. I understand and know you are in a very tough predicament. I am here to help however I can."

Corinne had probably said those words, or words just like them, to many others, and certainly felt the sincerity in every breath of them.

"Thank you. I'm really not quite sure what to do. It was my plan to go to college, probably in the United States, when I finished up school here. However, I hadn't thought too much about it just yet. I just knew it was what I would do when the time came. I was going to start looking into schools this spring, and then...well, the plan was to start this fall," said Gabrielle.

"If there's one thing I've learned about life it's that making plans is great on paper, but you can't plan for what you don't know is coming. It's okay though. We will get this figured out."

They continued to talk for almost an hour, getting to know one another. Corinne was a social worker who was only five years older than Gabrielle, but she seemed to have a world of experiences already. Gabrielle learned that she was married with three daughters and was living in Florida while her husband and girls were back in Canada. She has been in Florida living with and taking care of her sick aunt.

Corinne's mother had already divorced their father by the time he and Elodie met and had Gabrielle. As far as Corinne knew, Gabrielle was the youngest...that he had no more children after her. They talked about Edgar, but Gabrielle was careful not to say too much, not knowing how close they were or whether or not

Corinne would repeat anything to him. She was starting to trust Corinne.

"I am not as comfortable living under Edgar's roof as I thought I'd be. It is safe to say that I'm looking forward to finishing school."

"Well, Gabrielle," Corinne started, "I plan on being in Florida for a while. My husband and our daughters will eventually move down here with me since we're not sure how long I'll be here. I miss them."

"I bet you do. That must be hard on your family to be so far apart," said Gabrielle.

"Yes, it is very difficult to be away from my girls. I am sure they are growing so fast, and I am missing out on that. But enough about that. Tell me, have you decided what to do about the baby? Are you keeping it?" Corinne finally asked the question Gabrielle had been expecting her to ask. She was a bit surprised it took so long to broach the subject, but at the same time, she learned through their conversation that Corinne had tact.

"I will have the baby, but I feel it is only right to put it up for adoption so we can both have the chance at a good life. A life I simply can't give it at this stage, and one that will let me focus on my own goals," said Gabrielle. "I was also raised Catholic, and abortion goes against my belief system. None of this is the baby's fault, you know?" Gabrielle had put a lot of thought into her decision, mostly while tossing and turning at night and often when tuned out during school. Even though she had known from the beginning that this was the only right choice for her, she still had to weigh all of her options and follow her heart with its decision.

"How about this...what if you come here at the end of the summer, say in September, while you can still travel and to ensure plenty of time to look at schools and arrange the adoption. Also, just in case the baby has any plans on coming early. That way, you can take some time to look at colleges while you're here, then have the baby, and I can help you figure out the adoption process. Since I was a social worker in Canada, I have a few connections down here that I can call upon"

Gabrielle was overwhelmed by Corinne's offer. Not only because Corinne didn't have to put herself in this position of responsibility, yet still chose to, but mostly because for the first time Gabrielle knew what it was like to have a sister. The unconditional love completely caught her off guard.

"I wasn't expecting you to offer all of this, Corinne. I hadn't even thought of it. Are you sure?" Gabrielle asked, silently praying and thanking God for bringing her this solution.

"Yes, I most certainly am. I think it will work out for the best for everyone. Do you want me to talk to Edgar about it?"

"If you wouldn't mind? I think he might be more open to the whole idea if he hears it from you. At the same time, he knows I want to go to college and the United States has great schools, so it shouldn't be too much of a surprise to him. Besides, he is also the one who told me to call you. I think his transfer comes up this summer, too, and he's moving over there anyway. I don't know when he plans to leave Germany though. He tends to spring things on me." Gabrielle thought back to the day of their drive to the lake. She shuddered and closed her eyes for a moment before refocusing on her conversation with Corinne.

"Let me take care of telling him. You just focus on taking care of yourself. Call me whenever you need to," said Corinne. "I can't wait to meet you, and please have faith in God that everything will work out for the best."

"You have no idea what all of this means to me. I never knew what it was like to have a sister, but now I know. Thank you so much, especially for talking to Edgar for me."

After they hung up, Gabrielle began to feel a semblance of excitement about her future again. She had made the phone call before school, and was now running a little late, plus she missed the chance to walk with Sarah and Donna. But, with her renewed hope, she was able to pick up the pace and arrive at school not long after the first bell rang. The teacher didn't question her when she came in and sat at her desk, ready for class.

WHILE SARAH KNEW about Gabrielle's predicament, they had yet to tell Donna. Gabrielle was concerned about too many people finding out. She wasn't sure what the ramifications would be, and news like a pregnant teenager would spread like wildfire around school. Telling Sarah had been so emotional and unexpected, and though Gabrielle knew that Donna might feel hurt if she kept it secret from her, she also needed more time.

Figuring Donna would understand, even if she felt left out, Gabrielle waited until she found the right time and the privacy to do it.

That time came later that week when they were in the stairwell having lunch. It was actually Donna who tentatively broached the subject.

"Are you okay, Gabrielle?" asked Donna. "You've been missing some school, and seem distracted lately. I'm worried about you."

Sarah and Gabrielle exchanged looks, and Gabrielle knew this was probably the best moment to say something.

"Well, I'm not really okay, but I will be. I haven't had the right chance to tell you, and Sarah only knows because we live in the same building..."

"Knows what?" Donna looked back and forth between her two best friends.

"She found me crying one night last week," Gabrielle continued. "It turns out...well...it turns out I'm pregnant."

Gabrielle let her words hang in the air like a kite on a long string stretched far out into the sky. That was exactly how she had perceived this pregnancy, but with each day that kite's string was reeling in her reality, bringing it closer and closer until it began to sink in.

"Oh, my God!" gasped Donna. "And you knew about this?" Donna was facing Sarah now.

"I found her outside our building crying one night. After she told me, she spent the night at my place. It was a rough night, and I'm just thankful I could be there for her." Sarah put her arm around Gabrielle's shoulder.

"I totally understand. I really do," said Donna. "I can't imagine all the thoughts that are going through your head. What are you going to do? "

"As it turns out, Edgar told me that he and I have a sister I didn't know about. Can you believe I have a sister? She lives in Florida, and we spoke recently by phone." Gabrielle quickly diverted the conversation to Corinne in anticipation that it would deter other questions about the pregnancy, answers to which she could not share with Donna. Not now, and possibly not ever.

Donna shook her head and looked at Sarah to see if she knew this, too.

"That is news to me!" Sarah assured her. "Really? You have a sister?"

"Well, it gets better...if there is a better in all of this, it's because of Corinne. That's her name. She invited me to go stay with her in Florida at the end of the summer. I'll have the baby there. She was a social worker in Canada, so she can help with making the connections I need in Florida and all of the adoption details."

The more Gabrielle spoke about it, the more everything started to feel like what was becoming her new normal. Having a plan made it easier not only to explain to people, but as her own coping mechanism.

"I need to move into your building! I missed out on all of this? The baby? A sister?" Donna tucked the wrapper from her sandwich into her brown paper bag and whistled quietly before saying, "Gabrielle, the most important thing is that you have a plan and you're going to be okay. You know that if there's anything you need, you can ask me, too."

The three girls hugged just as the bell went off. Saved by the bell, Gabrielle thought, relieved that Donna did not have the chance to ask more questions.

"You two are the best friends anyone could have," Gabrielle said. "I really think you are the best thing that happened to me since I moved here. I don't know what I would do without you."

"Okay, enough of this," Sarah said. "Let's go to class and get this school year over with!"

Laughter echoed throughout the stairwell as they made their way through the door to their next class. For the first time in weeks, Gabrielle felt a sense of lightness. As she put her books down on her desk, she realized how long it had been since she laughed, and hoped that she would find opportunities to do so more often.

OVER THE WEEKEND Edgar let Gabrielle know that he had spoken to Corinne. "It is not my idea of a solution, but Corinne knows what she is doing and will take care of this. I will make your flight and whatever other arrangements." He was halfway out the door while talking to Gabrielle. Essie, Stella, and Emmanuel were at the PX, so Gabrielle was relieved that he was leaving for the base, too. She still did not trust being alone with him.

"Okay," was all she said before he left.

Gabrielle knew that all Edgar really had to do was to ensure she got on a plane to Florida later that summer. She thought about the irony of how the actions he had to take, and especially the action he had taken that led to all this, were all relatively short for him, and yet they were impacting her for the rest of her life. She didn't think she would ever fully be able to wrap her head around the situation. At the same time, she knew on some level that she didn't necessarily want to understand it. All she could ever hope for would to someday be able to forgive him, because with forgiveness she knew she would set herself free. But that, she knew, would take a very long time.

I

THE FIRST TIME Gabrielle met Edgar was in Haiti, and only two years before she got on the plane to Germany. She was visiting their father after a decade of being estranged from him. Elodie had encouraged Gabrielle's father to not only make an effort to get to know his daughter, but to also start helping to support her. Haitian single mothers were not guaranteed help from the father of their children, and were more often than not left to raise their children on their own, with little to no financial assistance. Elodie was only seventeen when she, too, became pregnant. She had been left on her own to support Gabrielle with only the help of her own mother.

Elodie had met Gabrielle's father while he was on assignment as a photographer. Like Gabrielle, Elodie was striking. She had also bypassed the gawky, awkward stage that so many teenage girls experience and went right from being twelve to being beautiful. Her Indian-like features caught the attention of many men, and Gabrielle's father was no different. He was debonair and his mysterious role of being a photographer gravitated Elodie, and many other women, toward him. He quickly gained the approval of Elodie's family, especially her aunt, who let him take Elodie back to the capital city to live with him. He was smitten with Elodie, and in turn, she was starry-eyed and very attracted to the older man with stature and an obvious passion for his work.

He took Elodie, his new prized possession, and deflowered her. What Elodie hadn't seen coming was that when she was seven months pregnant, he asked her to go back to her hometown so she could be with her family when Gabrielle was born. In her youthful innocence, Elodie conceded and returned to her family, believing he only wanted the best for her. By the time Gabrielle was born two months later, he had already replaced Elodie with another woman who had even moved into his house.

Devastated, Elodie had no place to go with Gabrielle. She stayed in her hometown for a short time before leaving Gabrielle with her mother while she returned to the capital city to make a living.

Gabrielle inherited Elodie's beauty, both attracting the wanted and unwanted attention of men. The difference was, Gabrielle learned early on that she didn't want the kind of attention her mother evoked from the opposite sex. She wanted respect. She wanted her fairytale. She wanted Benji.

Throughout the years, Elodie had been able to survive through several tumultuous relationships with married men. She owned her own store that sold miscellaneous goods. Gabrielle's father stopped providing for her except for the rare occasion that he stopped by to say hello and to give Elodie a few dollars. Eventually, when Jacques was in the picture, he took a stand and told Gabrielle's father to either financially take care of her or stop coming over. He chose the latter. By then, Gabrielle was old enough to grasp what was happening and since that day, she always wondered if her father had been relieved to be let off the hook. It was also in that moment that she gained a new found respect for Jacques. She saw the side of the man that Elodie seemed to love, and it made sense to her. Even if it didn't strengthen Gabrielle's and his relationship past what it was, it did let her see him in a better light.

It was the conflict between the two men and Elodie's dependence on them that opened Gabrielle's eyes to the realization that she wanted to be independent. She made a vow to herself that she would be self-sufficient and able to support herself without the help of a man. To her, it didn't ruin her fairytale vision of romance; in fact, it strengthened it. From that day forward, her journal had been filled with promises to herself that she would benefit from an education and eventually be able to be on her own. It was this promise that drove her, that got her out of bed every morning, and kept her up late doing homework at night. And, it was finding out that she was pregnant that made her realize exactly what Corinne had told her. She could plan all she wanted, but life has its plan for you, too. She just couldn't believe that God had anything to do with this plan.

I

CORINNE AND GABRIELLE exchanged letters weekly because it was less expensive than a phone call. Sometimes she mailed her letters to Corinne when she went to the mailbox with a letter to Benji. Other times, she gave the envelope with the Florida address to Edgar to mail. It was a passive way of letting him know that she was in touch with Corinne on a regular basis. In the back of her mind, she hoped that Edgar's knowing this would help to keep him, well, to keep him in line. His anger around the apartment tended to come in bursts and was often unpredictable. Sometimes she was the target; sometimes it was Essie or Emmanuel. Stella seemed to be the only one who wasn't on the receiving end, although, she was often in the room to witness them.

Gabrielle had yet to find out who had read her journal, but had taken to keeping it hidden in the bathroom in the cabinet under the sink behind the box of sanitary pads she would probably never use. She took to sitting on the bathroom floor and writing while the water in the shower ran. No one questioned why she was taking longer showers, and she at least felt like she had some of her privacy back while Stella was there.

THERE WERE STILL days when Gabrielle missed Benji to the point of tears. Days when her heart sank and she didn't think anything would be able to retrieve it. Donna and Sarah hadn't had boyfriends yet, so they weren't very empathetic of her situation. They listened as Gabrielle told them of the long walks she took with Benji and how they went to the movies every weekend. It was when she tried to explain to them what it was like to kiss him in the dark movie cinema that they tuned out. She finally stopped talking about it, and only found comfort in her journal and in her letters to Corinne.

She had told Corinne about Benji when they first talked, and continued to tell her more in her letters. However, she never mentioned Benji in the letters to Corinne that she knew she would be giving to Edgar to mail for her. She had heard that an envelope could be opened with steam and resealed.

"What? You're kidding? I guess it makes sense, though" said Gabrielle. The girls were walking to school and Gabrielle had asked them to wait a moment while she ran over to the mailbox to drop her letters in it.

"I've seen my father do it," said Donna.

"That's kind of creepy," said Sarah. "Don't you think?"

"Well, he had good reason to steam open the one I saw, but I'm sure there are plenty who don't!" said Donna.

Gabrielle was left wondering if Edgar actually steamed open her letters to Corinne, read them, and then resealed and mailed them. She wasn't sure he would go to all of that effort, but she had lost faith in the person she thought he was. The man she first saw was the one who would open doors to her future through world travel and grand opportunities, not the one who would shut down her world in the longest five minutes of her life. The bruises on her wrists had healed by now, but the deeply embedded emotional scar was what remained. Those defining moments were a blur to her now because her conscious mind wouldn't allow them to be drummed up, other than her view out the windshield as she laid back on the driver's seat of the station wagon. She remembered taking herself to a mental safe place—the place where she and Benji were at their tree—but even those thoughts she managed to shake from her mind because she didn't want to blend the two together. What was left were her unanswered questions for God and how He could allow such turmoil in her life despite the faith she always had in Him.

"We better pick up the pace; the bell is about to ring," said Sarah.

Once inside their classroom, and with books laid on their desks, the three sat down just in time for the echo of the bell throughout the school. It was a sound that Gabrielle welcomed every time she heard it. School was her escape now, not the tree with Benji, not her bedroom in her mother's house, and certainly not driving lessons with Edgar. They hadn't gone for a drive since that day, but the day she still looked forward to was the one when she would earn her driver's license. It was on her list to talk to Corinne about when she moved to

Florida. Having her license, she knew, would be one of her first steps toward the independence and freedom she vowed to be the gift she owed herself.

Chapter Twelve

BY THE TIME spring arrived and Gabrielle finished her last day of school, Stella was prepared to return to her hometown to pick up the pieces of her life that Essie couldn't help her with. Gabrielle gathered that she had learned the same lesson: that Essie and Edgar's home was not a place to escape to in order to find life's answers or to follow dreams. That what was perceived as opportunity had the tendency to backfire under their roof.

Nor did Gabrielle and Stella ever discuss Essie and Edgar's marriage again, but she did sense increased tension between Essie and Stella, which she could only imagine was the result of Stella questioning Essie. Gabrielle had distanced herself emotionally from the family and was focused on finishing out the school year and packing for her own move.

Grateful to have the school year behind her, Gabrielle was just starting to show, but with the magic of strategic dressing, she had been able to camouflage the developing roundness of her belly with specifically cut tops. She was certain that other than Sarah and Donna, none of the other students found out or else the gossip would have been unbearable.

Her volleyball coach knew, and sympathized, but was also disappointed because she had been counting on Gabrielle's skills and height on the court. The principal, and Edgar for that matter, ruled against Gabrielle traveling with the team earlier that year since she wouldn't be playing, and because of her "medical excuse."

"Hey, I know!" Gabrielle said as she walked home with Sarah. Donna had already parted ways at her street. "Let's go over to the pool hall tonight. We can hangout and celebrate being done with school."

"I don't know if I'm allowed...," said Sarah.

"Ask your mom. We won't stay out late. It's fun to watch them shoot the ball around the table."

"Okay, I'll ask. Sounds fun!"

AT SEVEN O'CLOCK Gabrielle met Sarah in the lobby of their building and they walked over to the pool hall. Gabrielle knew that Edgar would be there, as she had broached the subject and asked permission during dinner an hour earlier.

When Gabrielle opened the front door to the pool hall, the warm, testosterone-filled air greeted them. In some ways, it reminded Gabrielle of the evening air on the streets of Haiti when some of the men wore tank tops and strolled the streets to be seen, hoping to meet a new lady friend.

In the pool hall on base, the only source of lighting came from the fixtures hanging above each of the pool tables and the one at the bar across the room. Smoke swirled around the far pool table, illuminated by the hanging light above it; however, Gabrielle was relieved to see an oscillating fan that managed to blow most of it away, keeping the smoke from the front of the room.

"We can sit here...on the couch," Gabrielle pointed to the long couch against the wall.

"Let's get something to drink first," suggested Sarah, who was already gravitating toward the bar-tender.

As she followed Sarah, Gabrielle spotted Edgar out of the corner of her eye. He had left the apartment about ten minutes earlier than Gabrielle. She could feel the same one eye on her that had been on her the few other times she'd been there the past fall. His watchful eye only added to her craving of independence every time she sensed it.

"I'll have a root beer," Sarah stated to the bartender in her most bold voice.

"Going all out, huh?" Gabrielle joked, then looked at the bartender and said, "I'll have the same. Thank you." The bartender winked at her and went to grab two cold bottles from the refrigerator behind him.

"Here you go young ladies. No need to show me ID," he joked.

When they settled into the couch with their root beers, Gabrielle explained some of the rules of pool to Sarah, who hadn't a clue what the men were doing with the long cue sticks and colorful, numbered balls.

"They get to keep shooting until they miss putting a ball in the pocket," said Gabrielle.

"What? Their pocket? Wouldn't that be cheating?"

"Oh, my goodness! No! Not their pant pockets. The pockets are the holes in the table where the balls are supposed to..."

Right then the door opened, creating a stream of light across the floor and in front of their feet. Gabrielle looked up, and though the light was bright and the doorframe was only filled with a silhouette, she immediately knew who it was.

"Gabrielle?" the deep, recognizable voice asked.

Sarah looked at the man in the doorway then back at Gabrielle, who was smiling broadly.

"Yes, it's me. Hello," said Gabrielle. She knew those muscles. The tight shirt. The strong facial features. "Sarah, this is Peter. Peter, I'd like you to meet my friend, Sarah," said Gabrielle.

Sarah reached her arm out to shake Peter's hand. He stepped into the pool hall and let the door close behind him, and though he shook Sarah's hand, it was Gabrielle he looked at.

"Haven't seen you here in a while," he said to Gabrielle as he released Sarah's hand.

"Yes, I know. I got busy with school. We just finished today, so we came here celebrating."

"By drinking root beer, I see!" Peter grinned and Gabrielle melted into the couch. She couldn't place what it was about him that she was so attracted to, other than that he was a breath of fresh air whenever he showed up.

"Yes, well. Edgar is here." Gabrielle nodded her head in Edgar's direction.

"Ah, yes. Edgar the ogre."

Gabrielle and Sarah giggled until they heard Edgar on the other side of the room. "I heard that, Peter!" Sarah laughed harder, but Gabrielle managed to stifle hers. Peter simply turned and grinned at Edgar.

"Well, nice to see you, and to meet you, Sarah." Peter went over to Edgar's table and slapped him on the back and shook his hand.

"How on God's great earth do you know him?" Sarah asked. Her eyes were as big as saucers as she watched Peter walk away. She hadn't taken them off him while asking Gabrielle her question.

"From here. We met a few times last fall. He tried to buy me a beer, but Edgar put a quick stop to that. It embarrassed the heck out of me," whispered Gabrielle. She was certain Edgar had supersonic hearing.

"I bet." Sarah finally took her eyes off Peter and took a sip from her bottle that she had placed on the table next to her. "Too bad he's not your boyfriend."

"That would never fly as long as I'm under Edgar's roof. Besides, no one can replace my Benji. But, I must say, Peter is not only one of the nicest guys I've ever met, he also has something about him. Can't explain it."

"Oh, you don't have to. I get it."

Gabrielle was surprised when Peter made his way back to the couch, beer in hand, and sat down next to her. Instinctively, she crossed her arms over her belly.

"So, how have you been? We missed you around here. Only ones who come in here are just a bunch of smelly men," said Peter.

"I've been good. Some days are better than others. This is Sarah's first time here, so I was explaining the rules of pool to her." Gabrielle tilted her root beer toward Sarah.

"A first-timer? Well, don't let anyone here offend you. They're all sheep in wolves clothing," Peter grinned.

"Don't you mean the other way...," Gabrielle started.

"Shhhh!" Peter said. "Don't tell her."

Gabrielle and Sarah laughed, but when Gabrielle looked up to see Edgar staring at them, holding tightly to his cue stick, she toned it down to a very, very low roar.

The cracking noise of someone making a break shot filled the room. Gabrielle, Sarah, and Peter all watched as the balls scattered around the table with a few landing in pockets.

"So, now what?" Sarah asked.

"Now he gets to keep shooting as long as the balls keep going in a pocket...except the white one. That is the one he uses to hit the other balls, and it has to stay on the table. That is called the cue ball," explained Peter.

"It's like I told you, except I forgot to mention the thing about the white ball. Uh, the cue ball," said Gabrielle.

"This seems awfully complicated," Sarah sighed.

"Naw, it's easy. Want me to teach you?" Peter offered.

"Really?" Sarah's face lit up.

"Sure, grab a few cue sticks from the rack, and I'll set up a table. Gabrielle, do you want to play, too?"

"No thank you. I prefer to observe than play," said Gabrielle.

She watched as Peter and Sarah moved around the table. He often leaned over her, showing her how to make the best shot by the way she angled her cue stick.

Part of Gabrielle was jealous. She wondered what it would be like to have Peter leaning over her, feeling him pressed against her while he taught her how to master the game.

There was another side of her though that kept her stationed on the couch. The side that feared the touch of a man. The fear of feeling his breath on her neck while he spoke to her and instructed her on the next shot. The fear that she would overreact and pull away. Her instincts knew she was not ready for those experiences.

And so, she sat on the couch and sipped at her root beer, only occasionally glancing at Edgar...until one last request from Peter brought up a level of bravery within her.

"Are you sure you don't want to try? Just one shot?" he asked with an extra twinkle in his eye...a twinkle that came with a dash of pleading.

It was his final trick up his sleeve, his smile, which was enough to entice her to throw caution to the wind.

"Okay, one shot!" she said as she stood and walked over to the table. Sarah handed her the cue stick she had been using and went to stand on the other side of the table.

"Okay, lean in like this," Peter instructed. "Then angle yourself this way," he said as he took hold of the middle of her cue stick and positioned it toward the white ball in the middle of the table. There was a red one that he was apparently aiming for. "Now, pull it back like this and keep your elbow tight to your waist." He loosely held his hand on her waist as he spoke.

Gabrielle looked up at him and smiled. She could smell the cologne on his neck and a hint of beer in his breath as he spoke.

"Pay attention to the ball on the table," he teased her.

She felt her cheeks flush and she quickly looked back down at the table. "Sorry," she said and her body tensed up again.

"I'm just teasing you. It's okay, really." His natural way of comforting her would have startled her if she didn't already know his personality.

"Okay, I'm ready," she said.

"Great. Now, pull back, like this, and...shoot!"

The cue stick hit the white ball. The white ball hit the red ball. And in a matter of seconds, the red ball swished the inside of the corner pocket.

"You did it!" exclaimed Peter.

Gabrielle turned and gave Peter a high-five. "My first pool shot, ever!"

"Very good. Now let's try..." Peter was interrupted by Edgar's finger poking him on the back of his shoulder.

"That's enough for tonight. One shot was all she needed," Edgar said, putting himself between Peter and Gabrielle.

"Just one...," Peter started.

"Nope. She is done here." Edgar turned to Gabrielle, who didn't need to be told to go sit back down on the couch. She went and joined Sarah, who had apparently seen Edgar walking over to the table and went to take her seat on the couch in anticipation of trouble.

"Okay. Sorry. We were just having fun. Nothing else," Peter said with his hands held up as though he was showing a police officer he wasn't armed.

Edgar went back to his table, not seeing Peter turn and wink at the girls. He continued to shoot the rest of the balls on the table until they were all in their respective pockets; that is except the white one.

WHEN ENOUGH TIME had passed to let the tension ease, Gabrielle suggested to Sarah that they leave. Sarah's parents had set a ten o'clock curfew, and she knew Edgar would want her home by then, too. They said goodbye to Peter and let Edgar know they were leaving. During their walk home, they didn't say much except that they agreed that Peter was someone special. Not a word was spoken about Edgar's behavior, but Sarah had yet to, nor would she again after the night Gabrielle confided in her, go over to Gabrielle's apartment. Gabrielle quietly understood why, and had she been in Sarah's shoes, she wouldn't have either.

Back at home, in the once again solitude of her bedroom, Gabrielle reflected on the pool hall and the tables surrounded by men with one goal: to place all the balls, except the white one, in the pockets. She thought about how the men filled their evenings poetically striking at balls with a cue stick and wondered about the wives and girlfriends waiting at home for them. Inspired by the thought of their bodies moving about the table, seeking the right opportunity for a pocket, and wondering about the reasons they escaped to the pool hall in the first place, she opened to the next blank page in her journal and picked up her pen off the nightstand.

Today was the last day of school. Sarah and I went to the pool hall where we saw Peter. Of course Edgar had to make a scene, so we didn't get to play much. I can't wait to be gone from here. To be in Florida where I can have this baby and we can both move on with our lives. I pray every day that God has a plan to make all of this up to me somehow. Someday, perhaps, I will be able to look back and some of it will make sense, but I can't imagine parts of what has happened will ever make sense to me.

Chapter Thirteen

AS SPRING TURNED into early summer, Gabrielle spent less time with Donna and Sarah and more time planning for Florida. Edgar had bought her plane ticket, which would send her off on September first, exactly fourteen months after leaving Haiti in the first place. The letters back and forth between Corinne increased, and the two also spoke on the phone once a week. The plans were falling into place as fast as Gabrielle's belly was growing. Her regular visits to the clinic ensured that both she and the baby were doing well.

"You're lucky you were spared morning sickness," the nurse told her during one of her last visits. "A lot of women have it pretty bad."

"I know. I was especially glad I didn't have it during school," said Gabrielle. "That would have been the worst."

"Well, everything looks good. We will send the reports to the hospital in Florida. Good luck with everything." The nurse put Gabrielle's chart down and held the door open for her as she left the exam room.

That evening when she was sitting on the couch with Emmanuel, both reading books, he finally looked up at her and asked, "What's with your belly growing, Gabrielle. It's big!"

Gabrielle had to laugh, but at the same time questioned just how she would tell him. "Well, there's a baby growing in there. That's why I'm moving to Florida to be with your Aunt Corinne. She's going to help me with it."

"A baby? Does that make me an uncle?" His innocence touched Gabrielle deeply.

"Well, yes, I guess so."

"Neat!"

Gabrielle smiled down at Emmanuel who went back to reading his book.

Kids, she thought, as she turned the page of her own book. That was much easier than telling anyone else.

THE ONLY THING missing from the not-so-perfect picture and her next set of plans was Elodie. Gabrielle didn't know how to tell Elodie she was pregnant; the shame and embarrassment kept her from doing so. She knew Edgar would never tell her. She also knew that if she kept it a secret for too long, her mother would be that much more hurt when she eventually found out. It was a decision Gabrielle struggled with daily, and it was apparent in the reduced number of letters and phone calls she made to Elodie. Even when Gabrielle did call home to her mother, the brevity of the conversations magnified the fact that she was hiding something.

Eventually, Gabrielle at least told Elodie of her plans to go to Florida to visit her sister. Gabrielle had already spoken to her mother about Corinne, telling her how happy she was to know that she had a sister and that they were bonding. Sensing a pang of jealousy from Elodie over it, Gabrielle toned down her excitement, but also knew there was really nothing Elodie could do about it. Gabrielle and Corinne's connection was a very different one than the one she had with her mother. Corinne had become Gabrielle's new sounding board, not that her mother had ever been a very solid one, but Gabrielle was starting to realize that Elodie had done the best she could under their circumstances. On some level, both Gabrielle and Elodie understood this.

BY THE MIDDLE of June, Gabrielle was growing more and more excited about leaving Germany behind for Florida. Corinne had sent her a packet full of pamphlets from adoption agencies and booklets from colleges. Gabrielle spent a lot of time pouring through the pamphlets and dreaming of her future now that she was done with school. She put most of her focus into the business programs, as they were what she was drawn to the most. She knew that honing her business skills and earning her bachelor's degree in it were going to be critical to her success. She also toyed with the idea of going into elementary education since she loved being in the classroom and wanted to impact the lives of youths.

"I'm very proud of you for looking into the business programs," Corinne had told her on the phone one Saturday afternoon. "With your scholastic history, you should be a shoe-in anywhere you apply. I think you are going to love Florida, too. The climate will be much more like what you were used to Haiti, rather than those cold and snowy German winters."

"You are definitely right about that," said Gabrielle as she shook the image by the lake on that cold and bitter day from her mind. "I'm also curious about education. Teaching elementary kids would be fun. I'm just not sure how to blend the two, so maybe I can meet with the schools' counselors to help sort through it all. I hope I have at least a couple of weeks to look around at different campuses before the baby comes. That is if I can waddle around okay."

"I'm certain that can be arranged. I will look into it for you because some of the schools might have better education programs," said Corinne. "Just wrote it down. Anything else we need to think about?"

"What about the adoption agency? Did we decide on the one with Mrs. Donaldson?" Gabrielle was looking at her own checklist of items to talk to Corinne about. The number of details to address seemed endless.

"I think her agency has the best reputation here. Are you comfortable with that?" asked Corinne.

"Yes, I trust your instinct. Have you set an appointment to meet with her?"

"I did. We're set for three o'clock on Monday, September eighth, so just a few days after you get here. It's not too far from the house, either."

"Okay, great." Gabrielle added the appointment to her calendar. "I have one more question. It's not on the to-do list though."

"What is it?" asked Corinne.

"Do you think I will be able to hold the baby? You know, at least for a moment?" Gabrielle still wasn't sure whether or not that would be a good idea.

The baby she had always imagined holding for the first time had been Benji's. She thought of him pacing in the waiting room until the nurse came out with their baby wrapped in a blue or pink blanket and telling him everything went well—that Gabrielle was doing fine. She imagined the look of joy on his face when he saw their child for the first time. She even went so far as to imagine them picking out names.

Now all of that would only be a fantasy. She had no idea how he would react to her knowing that she had given birth to another man's child or if she could even gather the courage to tell him what had happened. The thought of how one short yet poignant event could turn her world so incredibly upside down left her emotionally numb most of the time.

"That's a good question for when you meet with Mrs. Donaldson. Write down all of your questions so you have a list when we go in," suggested Corinne, bringing Gabrielle out of her thoughts.

Gabrielle had learned to accept all of the assistance Corinne was giving her. It was not only welcomed, but it was something she was starting to grow accustomed to. She credited her mother for putting her in the Catholic school and Edgar for bringing her to Germany, but everything Corinne was doing for her was entirely selfless and unexpected.

When Gabrielle left Haiti, she had her future all figured out. She would finish school in Germany, attend college in the United States, and start working once she graduated. She could not have anticipated the literal and figurative bump in the road that she hit; but, she knew one day that hindsight would show her. In the meantime, she saw it as the impetus for Edgar telling her about Corinne, who had been instrumental in helping her not only find the colleges she could apply to but to help manage the baby bump that appeared in her road of life.

GABRIELLE ALSO DREAMED of her baby's future. Corinne had sent her ample information on adoption, how the adoption process worked, and even a pamphlet from the hospital where she would give birth in only a matter of months.

Gabrielle couldn't help but to think about how she would feel when the day came to give birth. Most of all, she wondered if she would even be able to see and hold her baby, even if for a moment, before the nurse would wrap it in a warm blanket and take it away to its new family. Whenever that thought was too overwhelming, she tapped into the future, a future even further down the road, and pictured her little boy or girl being taught how to ride a bicycle down the sidewalk or how to tie shoes by parents who loved every bit of him or her. She knew deep down in her core that there were parents out there waiting to provide her child with their love, their home, and who would give it their world.

I trust in you, God, that whoever takes my baby into their home will intuitively know how to raise it and care for it. When and if the time comes, I hope they will find the right words to tell their child the story of how a young, teenage girl became pregnant and loved her baby so much that she knew the best solution was to give it up for adoption with another family who would see to it that they had every opportunity in life it wanted.

These thoughts, written in her journal, were the ones that empowered Gabrielle in the moments when she asked herself whether or not she was doing the right thing. The reality for her was that her other choices were incomprehensible.

WHEN JULY 1, 1980 arrived, Gabrielle didn't expect anyone to pay attention to her eighteenth birthday. But, when Sarah and Donna invited her to Sarah's to bake a cake and open presents, she was very touched. They spread chocolate frosting on vanilla cake and covered their masterpiece in rainbow colored sprinkles. Sarah's mother poured them lemonade and when they were done eating two pieces of cake each, they rolled on the couch and claimed their bellies ached.

"You think yours aches? Try being as big and round as me and eating two pieces of cake," laughed Gabrielle. It was then when she felt a sudden pressure inside her belly. "What was that?" She looked down at her belly then up at Sarah's mother.

"Did the baby just kick?" Sarah's mother asked. "I bet that's all it was. Can I feel?"

Gabrielle nodded yes and Sarah's mom placed her hand on Gabrielle's stomach just as the baby gave another kick. "That's exactly what it is. The baby is probably doing jumping jacks with all that sugar you just fed it!"

"Wow. I haven't felt it kick that strong before."

Gabrielle realized in that moment the comfort she felt being at Sarah's with her friends for her birthday. Sarah's mother had been a source of motherly security when Gabrielle needed it most, and for that she was eternally grateful to her.

"WHAT TIME DO you leave next Friday?" asked Sarah a few weeks later.

"Mid-morning. I think my flight is around ten. I remember thinking we wouldn't have to get up too early to leave for the airport," said Gabrielle. They were sitting on the grass outside their apartment building waiting for Donna to come over.

"Are you nervous?"

"About what?"

"The baby, giving birth. All of it."

"I've been worried about labor pains and all of that. How do women pass several pounds of flesh in the form of a wiggly baby out of them? I can't imagine, but I guess I'll be finding out soon enough."

"Finding what out?" Donna asked as she approached.

"How painful childbirth is!" said Sarah.

"Oh, good Lord. I can't even fathom..." Donna sat down next to the girls. They were each dressed in shorts and T-shirts with their hair pulled back in ponytails. Anyone looking at them from a distance, and who didn't notice Gabrielle's expansive belly, would have thought it was a group of teenage girls giggling about boys and discussing current fashion trends, but certainly not a baby passing through their birth canal.

"Do you think it's a boy or a girl?" asked Sarah.

"I don't know, but Essie thinks it's a boy because I'm carrying it low."

"Well, you're so tall that your carrying it low is like someone else carrying it high. That must account for something?"

"I honestly don't know. I'm wondering if I'll even be told anything about him or her once it's born...or if I'll even be able to hold it before they wrap it up and take it off into the next room. I've heard that's what they do." Gabrielle, beginning to choke up, looked off into the distance.

"I'm sure your sister will see to it that you're in good hands. It'll be okay, I promise. I wish we could be there with you...or at least in the waiting room," Sarah gave Gabrielle a hug and pat her on the back. Gabrielle sighed deeply.

"I wish we could be there, too. Maybe someday we can come visit you in Florida," said Donna, trying to be as cheerful as possible. Both of their families were moving that fall, too, which Gabrielle found some level of solace in.

After drying her tears with her T-shirt, Gabrielle managed to smile and say, "I'm going to miss you two—the three of us hanging out like this. But, you know I'm a good letter writer!"

"I'll write you back; don't worry about that," Sarah said. "Besides, you'll be back after the baby's born to get your things. This isn't the end yet."

"We'll be gone already," Donna said. "I heard my parents talking the other night. I think we're moving at the end of September now."

"Well, we still don't leave until October. We'll see what happens." Sarah stood up and encouraged the other two to join her. "I'm tired of sitting. Let's walk over to the park. It'll be good for you, Gabrielle."

"My feet are swollen and hurting. You two go. I'm going to go upstairs. I still have a lot to do before next Friday. I'll see you tomorrow, though."

Sarah and Donna waved goodbye and made their way up the road. Gabrielle watched in envy of her two friends who still had a significant piece of their childhood. When they were out of sight, she went inside and pushed the button to the elevator that would take her to the apartment that soon enough she would no longer be calling home. Rather than doing the paperwork she had planned, she pulled out her pen and journal and captured her emotions in a poem.

Oh my heart
Nature is dressed up in her best fall attire
She is free, happy, and proud
But you, my heart, you revel in the darkness of the past
Thoughts of those dark days of life
Invade you and make life senseless
When dawn breaks and
The sun reveals its majesty in the clear sky
My heart, you close your eyes
And cry silently
Over your lost love,
Your solitude
Seems to be your most cherished friend
Cheer up, you need to do better
Seek happiness
Live your life
Live this life that is opening up to you
To offer you all these possibilities

Filled with tearful goodbyes and promises of letters, Gabrielle only saw Sarah and Donna twice again before leaving for Florida.

I

THE LAST TIME Gabrielle went to an airport to board a plane to Miami was considerably different. This time during the trip to the airport Gabrielle was left alone with her thoughts as Edgar sped down the autobahn in silence. Her luggage for the month ahead lay on the back seat. All of her other belongings were mostly packed in boxes so that when she returned it would be easy to finish up packing and leave Germany behind once and for all. She was limited in the amount of heavy lifting she could do, and Edgar and Essie hadn't helped, other than Edgar loading her luggage in the station wagon before they left for the airport. Not surprisingly to Gabrielle, they shrugged any duties to help her by indicating that she would be able to finish packing when she came back. Emmanuel offered to help, but there wasn't much he could feasibly do other than stack some boxes for her.

Gabrielle and Edgar had spoken only necessary words in the last several weeks, consisting primarily of the ones that had to do with her pending trip and Corinne's details on the other end. They hardly saw one another anyway. Gabrielle made sure to be out of the apartment or in her bedroom as much as she could. Other than meals, she had made herself scarce, which was harder to do when school let out.

She kept busy by taking Emmanuel to the park or on long walks until her feet couldn't bear treading any longer. Emmanuel had asked a few more questions about the pregnancy, some of which Gabrielle could only answer with, "When you're older, maybe I'll tell you."

One afternoon when Gabrielle was alone in the apartment with Essie, she decided to take the opportunity to confront her about her journal. Since the day she discovered someone had read it, she hid it in another place, but it still bothered her that someone knew all of her secrets.

They were in the kitchen putting away dishes when Gabrielle broached the subject as politely as possible. "Essie, I have a question for you. I want you to understand that it's not an accusation, but a question that I need answered." Gabrielle stopped drying the dish she had momentarily wrapped in a towel and looked at Essie.

"Well, what is it?" Essie, on the other hand, continued putting away the dishes.

"I noticed that someone read my journal. It was the night I spent at Sarah's a few months ago. The first night Stella arrived. The next day I noticed it because some papers had been shifted around and stuffed in the back of it," said Gabrielle.

"And you think it was me or Stella?" asked Essie.

"I didn't say that. I'm only asking to see if you know who might have read it. If Stella or anyone said anything to you. But, yes, if you did, I'd want to know that, too." Gabrielle continued to look right at Essie.

"I don't know anything about it. Sorry," said Essie coldly as she put a plate on its shelf. "Can you hand me that platter?"

"No, I can't." Gabrielle put the dish and towel down on the counter and left. With her increased hormones, her patience had decreased. Based on Essie's response, Gabrielle still didn't know if Essie had read her journal or not; what had frustrated her the most that day was the lack of empathy.

RIDING TO THE airport with Edgar, Gabrielle was glad Essie and Emmanuel had chosen to stay home. She didn't want an eventful goodbye, and Edgar didn't give her one at the airport either. He simply pulled up to the curb, ensured she had her ticket, and pulled her luggage from the station wagon.

"Wait here while I park the car," he said.

When he returned ten minutes later, he walked her to her gate and asked the attendant to help with the bag. Though Edgar's actions were helpful, Gabrielle couldn't help but notice how much they lacked emotion. He had stepped back and shut down on her weeks ago.

"Have a good flight," he said.

"Okay," was Gabrielle's only response.

When Edgar turned to walk away, Gabrielle sat down in one of the seats near the gate and looked out the window, just as she had fourteen months earlier, only this time with very different thoughts and wonderment about her future.

Chapter Fourteen

GABRIELLE WAS QUICKLY seeing the benefits of being pregnant. She was the first to board the plane, and the stewardesses fussed over her all the way from the gate to her seat, which was in the front of the plane. Ensuring she had a pillow, blanket, and magazines, they let her know that all she had to do was push the button over her head if she needed anything. Anything at all.

A VERY DIFFERENT scene unfolded back at the apartment. Edgar stepped out of the elevator and across the hall to their apartment. When he opened the door, he found

Essie standing in the hallway with her own bags packed.

"I know, Edgar," she said. "I know everything."

"What? What do you know?" Edgar's palms began to sweat.

"Gaby. The baby. All of it. I read it all in her journal, Edgar. Every bit of it." Essie's voice was shaking as she gripped tightly to one of her bags. The rest sat around her feet.

"When? How did you..."

"How, Edgar? Let's look at the hows. Like how long I've put up with your abuse. How long you were going to go without telling me. How long we pretended to be a family. What about those hows, Edgar?" Essie stood with her feet planted. She knew that her words, her voice, had to hold her up and to take even one step could throw her off her game.

"Essie. Please..." For the first time in his life, Edgar was speechless.

"I will send for the rest of my things once I'm settled."

"Where are you going? You can't do this! You can't leave me!" Edgar flung his arms in the air.

"Yes, yes I can and I am. And, where I am going is one thing I will not tell you right now. What I will tell you is that Gabrielle should be more careful about what she writes in her journals...or at least about letting people know she writes in one. She tipped me off. Claimed someone read it and cried about how it was full of all of her secrets." That last part Essie knew was a lie. "I found it cleaning the bathroom one day. Funny how both of you managed to keep this secret for so long while I continued to cook and clean for both of you. The lack of shame...incredible. It's just incredible to me."

Edgar stepped inside the apartment and closed the door. Essie watched his moves like a photographer in Africa eyeing a lion, waiting for the opportune moment to press the shutter release. When he didn't turn to lock the door, she took the moment to brush by him with her bags. As she reached for the door, he grabbed onto her arm. She pivoted and looked him right in the eye. "You don't want to do that, Edgar."

Succumbed, he let go. The echo of the door slamming followed, and when he looked up, Emmanuel stuck his head outside of his bedroom. "Daddy, what's going on?"

"It's okay. Mom is taking a short trip. But, we're going to be okay." Edgar sat on the couch and put his head in his hands, covering his furrowed brow. In a flash he stood up and went to the door, swinging it open.

"Essie!" he screamed at the top of his lungs, but the only one to hear him was the woman down the hall who was unlocking her door. She quickly retreated into her apartment. Edgar ran back inside and over to the window. When he looked down to the street, he saw a cab pulling out with Essie's silhouette in the back seat and screamed, "No!"

I

WHEN GABRIELLE EXITED the airport in Miami, the warm and humid air was a welcomed and familiar feeling. She looked around just in time to see a woman climbing out of her car and waving her arms. Gabrielle recognized Corinne right away. The same long legs, the same delicate and bronze skin.

"Oh, my goodness! Let me look at you!" Corinne said as she ran toward Gabrielle.

Gabrielle hugged tightly to the sister she never knew she had until recently. The sister who had been her saving grace for the past several months. And most of all, the sister who loved her unconditionally.

"Here, give me your bags. You shouldn't be carrying anything," Corinne said as she pulled Gabrielle's bags from her. "Let me put them in the car for you."

"Thank you," said Gabrielle. "I can't believe these swollen, aching feet have made it to Florida."

"I'm sorry I wasn't here to meet you at the baggage claim. I had an issue with my aunt that held me up for a few minutes. Let's get you back to the house and all settled in. You must be starving. I've got plenty of food, you just tell me what you want."

"With all the crazy cravings I've been having, that could change by time we get to your aunt's house!" Gabrielle climbed in the passenger side of Corinne's car. She was relieved to be back on the ground that would feel even better when she could put her feet up.

"Well, you look absolutely gorgeous." Corinne started the car and began pulling out of the parking spot. "Pregnancy does that to women."

"I don't feel very beautiful. I've seen plenty of pregnant women in my life, but now I can certainly appreciate all they go through. I was lucky that my first few months were pretty easy, but lately I seem to be doubling in size every time I wake up. I'm exhausted all the time, and of course, my feet can only hold me upright for so long."

"You're doing fabulous. But you're right; no one said being pregnant was easy. It's a wonder anyone has more than one child. Are you ready for your appointment on Monday?"

"I think so," said Gabrielle. "I guess the question is, are they ready for me?"

"I'm sure they are. This is what they do all the time. Mrs. Donaldson is a really neat lady; I think you'll be very comfortable talking to her. Even though I can't guarantee the rest will be easy, I can assure you that you'll like meeting her." Corinne turned the car into a driveway and announced to her aunt as they walked in the house that they were home. As they would soon find out, her aunt was in the back bedroom sound asleep.

ON MONDAY MORNING, Gabrielle woke up suddenly feeling very anxious about the appointment with Mrs. Donaldson. When she walked into the building with Corinne two steps behind her, all of her fears suddenly subsided. The building was colorful and welcoming. She could hear the click clack of high heel shoes in the distance, and a moment later a tall brunette turned the corner and greeted her. "You must be Gabrielle?"

"I am. Nice to finally meet you," said Gabrielle.

"My office is just here if you will follow me. I have all of your papers ready to review and will explain everything to you once we sit down. Can I get you a glass of water?" Mrs. Donaldson turned and looked at Gabrielle.

"Yes, actually, a glass of water would be wonderful. I hadn't thought I was thirsty until you mentioned it. Can my sister come with us?" asked Gabrielle.

"Of course she can; just follow me."

Once seated in Mrs. Donaldson's office, a young woman knocked on the door and brought Gabrielle and Corinne each a glass of water. After she left, Mrs. Donaldson didn't hesitate to get right down to business. She went over all of the papers with Gabrielle, explaining every step of the process. Gabrielle had chosen to have an open adoption. She wasn't exactly sure why, other than that if someday the child wanted to find her, she wanted him or her to be able to. A part of her was simply not ready to close the door completely.

"Has the father given up his rights?" Mrs. Donaldson surprised Gabrielle with her question.

"The baby's father...well, it was..." Gabrielle looked at Corinne, who had never asked about the father, but Gabrielle figured she would once she arrived in Florida. Looking back at Mrs. Donaldson, Gabrielle said, "My boyfriend lives in Haiti. This pregnancy is from something, someone, else. It was a rape."

"Oh. I'm so sorry," said Mrs. Donaldson.

"Thank you," said Gabrielle. She felt Corinne's hand touch her shoulder, but was too ashamed to face her just yet.

After going through all the papers, Mrs. Donaldson asked Gabrielle if she had any questions.

"The documents certainly lay everything out very well. I think I understand it all. The only question I have is whether or not I'll be able to hold or even see my baby after it's born." Gabrielle listened to the ticking of the clock on the wall while she waited for Mrs. Donaldson's answer.

"As long as the baby is healthy and okay, yes, they let you hold the baby for a moment. If for some reason, you don't want to, you certainly don't need to. Everyone seems to have different feelings about it. So, it all comes down to personal preference. But yes, if you would like to hold your baby, you may."

Gabrielle was finally able to face Corinne, and smiled at her when she heard she could hold her baby. She then looked back at Mrs. Donaldson. "Yes, I would like to."

"Okay, then we are all set. The hospital will notify me when you are admitted." Mrs. Donaldson closed Gabrielle's folder. "I certainly appreciate you coming to us. I'm sure it wasn't an easy decision."

Gabrielle and Corinne stood and shook hands with Mrs. Donaldson, who showed them back down the hallway to the front door.

During the drive home Corinne broke the silence. "Was it someone in the army who did this? The rape?"

"Yes, he's in the army. Is it okay if we don't talk about it though?"

"Of course," Corinne said. "But, if you ever want to talk, I'm here."

"I know. Thank you."

She hadn't lied to Corinne, Edgar was in the army. And Gabrielle couldn't bear to think of what Edgar would do if he found out she confided in Corinne. To add to it, she felt an exorbitant amount of shame already. She couldn't imagine what Corinne might think, if Gabrielle might have done something... She shook away the thought and watched the houses pass one by one as they drove home.

OVER THE NEXT several days, Corinne took Gabrielle to different college campuses nearby. She was able to meet with some counselors regarding the best direction to take. Her next step was to fill out applications, which seemed like a long and arduous task since she was tired most of the time. The baby was now due any day, and often times she woke up in the middle of the night wishing and praying that it was all just a nightmare. She was really with Benji on their honeymoon planning their family. She found that as the time grew closer to giving birth, the thought of Benji, and the child she fantasized they would have, came to mind more and more. She got to the point where these thoughts dominated all others and at times the ache she felt for him was even more unbearable than the aching feet that did their best to carry her around throughout the day.

"So, have you given more thought to which school you like best?" Corinne asked Gabrielle one morning over breakfast. Gabrielle was eating a large bowl of cereal with strawberries and blueberries on it.

"They all have pros and cons, so I think I'm going to apply to them all and see which ones accept me. After the baby is born, and my head is a little clearer, I will narrow it down and make a decision. The one thing I do know is that I will be grateful when this phase is behind me."

Gabrielle put her spoon down and looked out the window. She thought about how most mothers went through the nesting phase where they prepared the baby's room, had baby showers, bought baby clothes, and were picking out names. She missed out on all of that. It all could have been different. It all should have been different.

What had she done to let Edgar think all of this was okay to put her through? It was a question she had asked herself over and over again. She had gotten better at not letting her mind get carried away with its own version of responses. Instead she tried to think of something happier. Whether it was a memory from the past or a wish for the future, escaping the answers to that question meant keeping her sanity.

TWO DAYS LATER when Corinne was in the garden and Gabrielle was in the kitchen getting a glass of lemonade, she felt her water break. It dribbled down her legs and into a puddle on the floor. She looked down in an odd state of subdued panic. She reached forward and knocked on the window to get Corinne's attention, and when Corinne saw her waving to come inside, she put down her clippers and tore off her gardening gloves. When she arrived in the kitchen moments later, Gabrielle was saying, "We've got to go! We've got to get to the hospital!"

"Okay, Gabrielle. It's okay. Let me wash my hands real quick. Can you get to the car okay?"

"Yes, I think so. But hurry," said Gabrielle.

After washing her hands, Corinne rushed about the house grabbing a few items, such as Gabrielle's overnight bag. When she arrived at the car, Gabrielle was sitting in the front seat with her hand on the dashboard and her head straight ahead.

"Oh, my God. I'm so scared!" Gabrielle screamed.

"Take a deep breath, Gabrielle. It's all going to be okay. I promise. The hospital is very close," Corinne reassured her. She was right, and after only one red light, they pulled up in front of the emergency room.

Corinne hopped out of the car and ran to get an attendant, who grabbed a wheelchair and brought it out to the car. Between the two of them, they ensured that Gabrielle sat in the wheelchair. They pushed her inside where Corinne gave Gabrielle's information to the lady at the registration desk. When she was done, she went back to Gabrielle' side and held her hand.

"You're going to do just fine. You're such a brave girl, and I know you can do this." She was looking right in Gabrielle's eyes, and in that moment Gabrielle felt a sense of relief and even belief that she was going to find the strength to get through this.

They wheeled her into her room and closed the curtains around her. Nurses began to make preparations at the counters next to Gabrielle. She couldn't bring herself to look at the forceps or anything else that was metal for that matter. One of the nurses, a plump blonde, turned to Gabrielle and instructed her to breathe deeply. That would help. As the contractions grew closer together, the pain intensified, and shortly thereafter the doctor came in. Finally!

"Hello there, young lady. You picked a nice day to have a baby, didn't you?" He smiled a gentle smile at her. But all Gabrielle could do was scream as the next contraction came. The nurse came over to her side, and said, "Squeeze my hand if it helps. As tight as you want. I'm used to it."

Gabrielle took her up on her offer, and between squeezing the nurse's hand and screaming while another nurse blotted her forehead with a cool washcloth, it seemed that she might possibly make it through this delivery.

After five and a half hours of screaming, sweating, and gripping tightly to the nurse's hand, the doctor finally said, "Okay, Gabrielle. You're doing great! Can you give me one last good push? Just one should do it for you. Bring this baby into the world."

Gabrielle looked at him with uncertainty in her eyes, as though she was going to hold him to his promise, and with that she gave one last push along with another hearty scream. Her head tilted back as she looked up at the other nurse, the one holding a cold compress on her forehead, and it was in that moment when Gabrielle swore she saw an angel appear. For a brief moment, as she felt the baby make its way into the world, the excruciating pain subsided, and she suddenly felt a connection to God that she had never known before. *I did it. I gave birth. Thank you, God, that's over.* And, when the baby's cries filled the room, replacing her screams, she began to cry, too.

After the nurse cleaned up the baby, she wrapped it in a warm blanket and brought it over to Gabrielle. "I understand you wanted to be able to hold your baby. I can also let you know that it's a boy. A seven pound, eleven ounce healthy boy."

Gabrielle took the bundle in her arms and as a tear rolled off her cheek and onto the baby's cheek, she knew in that moment that they would be bonded forever, even though they were being separated. Almost as quickly as they put the bundle in her arms, another nurse came in and took the baby away. Gabrielle gave him a quick kiss on the forehead and whispered goodbye.

Gabrielle lay in bed, completely alone, and stared at the ceiling. Under her breath she whispered, "God grant me the serenity to accept the things I cannot change; courage to change the things I can; and wisdom to know the difference."

She closed her eyes and clenched her fists, adding, "Please find my baby a good home."

In her moment of privacy, Gabrielle silently named her son Philippe.

Several minutes later, Corinne slid the curtain open. "Can I come in? Are you doing okay?"

"Of course, please come in. I'm doing okay, I guess." Gabrielle really didn't know what else to say.

"You must be exhausted. But the doctor said everything went well. They told me it was a baby boy and that you got to hold him for a few moments. Were you fine with that?" Corinne's eyes were filled with tears and empathy.

Gabrielle nodded her head yes as she choked up, unable to form the words to describe what it had felt like to hold her baby.

A few days later, both Gabrielle and her baby boy went home. Except, she went to Corinne's aunt's home, and the baby went to his new adoptive family's home. Gabrielle wasn't told much about the family, other than that they came to pick him up. Mrs. Donaldson assured her that she would have been happy with the selection though.

When she was settled back in at Corinne's aunt's house, Gabrielle pulled out her journal. She thought about and wrote about family and what it meant to her.

> *My mother never married, and since I have a half-brother and a half-sister, and especially since Benji is apparently and quite possibly engaged to—or worse yet married to—somebody else already, I am left with a lot of questions for God.*
>
> *I just gave up my firstborn child for adoption. He is beautiful with the softest skin on earth. He smelled like*

heaven to me, and I am so grateful for the moment I was able to hold him in my arms. I will cherish that moment forever...praying every day for him. Though I am certain the family Mrs. Donaldson chose for him will give him their own special name, to me my son is Philippe.

Through all of this, especially this past year, I have decided that family can be a convoluted and complicated concept, and that what I know of family is far from my own fairytale picture of it. I still hope that someday I will have the chance to experience what a normal family should feel like. And, perhaps, just perhaps, someday I will be able to meet my son again...my Philippe.

Gabrielle went back and forth between this tainted version of marriage, and the fantasy that she would wake up from the nightmare of her last year, and find Benji by her side, living the life she always wanted. The life they had dreamed about together. At times, living in that fantasy world helped Gabrielle to keep her sanity. She used it as an escape from her harsh reality.

Chapter Fifteen

OVER THE NEXT few weeks Gabrielle oscillated between feeling grief and feeling relief. She spent most of her time wondering about Philippe and the new parents who brought him into their home. She couldn't help but imagine the mother bathing him and rocking him to sleep. She questioned if she had made the right decision about giving up her baby boy. Several possible scenarios played in her head, and she became convinced that he would have all the love, the care, a steady home, and everything else that she was unable to offer him. She trusted Mrs. Donaldson's experience and her selection in parents, and remembered her comment that Gabrielle would have been happy with the selected parents. She didn't try to hold back any tears when she felt overwhelmed with all conflicting emotions that came up. Corinne convinced Gabrielle that everything she was going through, all the thoughts and emotions, were normal. They were exactly what were to be expected.

"Trust me, Gaby, I have worked with young girls like you often," said Corinne. "Your loss will never completely leave you, but it gets better in time...all the pain, all the questions. Somehow life finds a way to continue on; I promise."

By the end of the next few weeks, Gabrielle was sleeping better and her body was starting to feel somewhat normal again after nine months of stretching and pulling and reshaping, not to mention the over five hours of labor it went through.

"My breasts are killing me!" Gabrielle told Corinne one morning. "Will this ever stop?"

"I'm so sorry, Gaby. It's one of those Mother Nature things that we can't really do anything about. However, I have read that sage tea helps to reduce milk production, which will help. We can pick some up if you want to try it."

Corinne was sitting amongst her aunt's flowerbed, pulling up weeds. They were outside in the garden while her aunt slept inside; Gabrielle was sitting on a bench reading a book. Being early fall, temperatures had cooled down slightly for Florida. One big difference Gabrielle had noticed since she had been in Florida was the variety of smells. Besides the pregnancy heightening her sense of smell, Germany's winter really didn't have much in the way of aromas, other than the occasional whiff of burning wood or the smell of meals being cooked at dinner throughout the apartment building. She could smell those in the hallways. The air in Florida, on the other hand, carried citruses, ocean breezes, and floral aromas, sometimes all at once. Every time Gabrielle ventured outdoors, she was treated to a Florida potpourri. Perhaps the thickness of the air held tightly to them, like a spider web catching moths. Even better, her skin was supple again, like it had been in Haiti. The dry winter of Germany left it craving the moisture it now found in Florida.

"Really? Sage? Who comes up with these things? But at this point, I'll try anything to relieve this pain," said Gabrielle as she crossed her arms tightly over her breasts in hopes the pressure would somehow help. On a subconscious level, she also meant the emotional pain. Tea sounded like just the resource that could perhaps help alleviate both.

"Well, let's try it then! I know a place in town that must sell it. We can stop by and pick some up." Corinne brushed her hands on her shorts, wiping the dirt from the garden that left fingerprints on the outer pockets. She brushed her forearm against her forehead, pushing back her matted hair that was drenched with sweat. "Let me go in and clean up. We can head down there before the afternoon thunderstorms come."

When Gabrielle and Corinne went inside, there was a message on the answering machine from Edgar. He sounded distraught, and hearing his voice rattled Gabrielle more than she expected it might. Her time away from Germany, and the distance between them, had given her breathing room; yet in the moment she heard his voice boom through the answering machine, she felt suffocated.

"This is Edgar. I need to let Gabrielle know that there is no need for her to come back to Germany. Essie left. It's a long story, and I won't get into it on this answering machine, but I need to let you know that I am leaving the army with an honorable discharge since my service is up and, well...no need to go into details other than to tell you that Emmanuel and I will be arriving in Florida in three weeks. I will arrange to have Gabrielle's things brought with us. We will see you then."

Gabrielle looked at Corinne, wanting to gauge her response; and yet, she didn't seem disturbed or bothered by the news. Instead, she went down the hall to her room to clean up for the drive into town. "I'll be ready in half an hour."

Gabrielle stood and stared at the answering machine. What did he mean Essie left? Where did she go? But most of all, why?

"Well, that's good news. You don't have to go back to Germany after all. Unless you wanted to?" Corinne was backing the car out of the driveway as she spoke.

"No, I really didn't want to. I may have been able to see Sarah one more time, but the thought of another big trip like that was daunting. For the first time in several months, I finally feel settled, like I'm getting back to my normal self again. A new normal, anyway." Gabrielle looked out the window at the perfectly manicured neighborhood. Everything was so colorful. She hadn't realized how much she missed warmth and colors. "If I were to get on a plane to anywhere, it would be to Haiti."

"You mean to see Benji?"

"Well, yes. Being here makes me feel like I'm in such close proximity to him. When I was at Edgar's, I was literally on the other side of the world. But here, I feel like he's just down the road. You know?"

"Yes, I can see that. But what if Sasha is right? What if he is seeing someone, or even more so, what if he's already married?" Gabrielle had learned that Corinne was very direct, but in a good way where she meant well.

"That's why I feel the need to go. I never received any letters from him, and it seems the only way I'll get the answers I need is by going there." Gabrielle had turned her attention back inside the car. She dug into her handbag and pulled out a picture of her and Benji. It was her favorite one. They were outdoors sitting on her front steps. She was wearing a sundress and leaning into him with her head on his shoulder. He had his arm around her and a smile on his face that always told her how much he loved her. A smile that was meant for only the time he spent with her. "Take a look at this. Is that not the epitome of love?"

Corinne had parked the car in the parking lot of the shop they were going to. She took the photo from Gabrielle's hand and looked down at it. "You two certainly make a beautiful couple. I just don't want to see you get hurt. But at the same time, you have a few more weeks before Edgar and Emmanuel arrive. And, I'm certain your mother would love to see you. Perhaps a trip to Haiti is the best medicine for you right now. You can find out the answers to your questions and move on with your life one way or the other. But first, let's go inside and get some of this tea so your breasts aren't hurting and leaking when you see him!"

Gabrielle couldn't help but to laugh. Corinne was right. Gabrielle's body was not quite the same as it had been the last time she saw Benji. With all that it had been through, she felt like she had aged five years. But, she agreed with Corinne that this trip could actually be the best medicine.

Later that afternoon, after pouring a mug of sage tea, she sat down with Corinne to make plans for her trip. The angst and tension that had filled her for months was suddenly replaced with butterflies in her stomach. Was she really going to see her Benji?

By dinnertime that evening, the plans had been made. Corinne readily contacted a friend who worked for a travel agency, and Gabrielle was set to fly out in three days. For the first time in ages, she was too excited to write in her journal when she went to bed. Instead, she tossed and turned and didn't fall asleep until after three o'clock in the morning.

It wasn't until ten o'clock the next morning that Corinne knocked on her door. "Time to get up, sleepy head! You have a lot to do to prepare for your trip."

The first phone call Gabrielle made that day was to her mother. One thing she tossed and turned about the night before was how she was going to tell Elodie about Philippe. On many levels, Gabrielle knew that at this point it was best to tell her in person. So when she made the phone call, and Elodie answered the phone, Gabrielle surprised her with the news that she would be there the day after next.

"Really? My baby girl is coming home?"

"Yes, but only for a few days." Gabrielle had intentionally set her stay for only a few days because not only was she not sure how things would go with Benji, but for many reasons she needed to be back in Florida before Edgar and Emmanuel arrived. They were coming to stay with Corinne and her aunt, and they had shipped all of her belongings ahead with their own items.

"This is such great news. I'll be sure your bedroom is ready."

"Thanks, momma," said Gabrielle before they hung up.

I

THE GLISTENING TARMAC on the runway in Port-au-Prince radiated heat under the belly of the airplane as the passengers deplaned. As promised, Elodie met Gabrielle at the gate.

"Oh, my goodness! Look at you! I can't believe you are here!" Elodie squeezed Gabrielle tightly.

"Hi, mom." Gabrielle hugged her back, and then pulled herself free to gather her belongings.

"Let's get you to the house. I'll make you something nice to eat for lunch, and you can fill me in on everything. It seems like we haven't spoken in ages."

Once at the house, Gabrielle brought her bags to her old bedroom. Nothing had changed; everything was still in its proper place. There was a huge part of her that felt comfort in being back in time, back in her old bedroom. And then there was another part of her that felt like she didn't know who the young girl was who grew up in that room. What had happened to her?

ONCE THEY WERE settled in and Gabrielle had had a bite to eat, she decided there was only one way to tell her mother about Philippe, and that was to just open up and say it.

"I have something to tell you. Please let me tell you everything, and when I'm done I'll answer questions. But, I can't promise that I can answer all of your questions." Gabrielle took a deep breath and looked at her mother who was looking back with wide eyes of anticipation. "As you might be able to tell, I have a few extra pounds on me." Gabrielle noticed Elodie looking her up and down.

"A few, yes, I can see that, but what does that have to do with anything?" Elodie sat up straighter on the couch.

"Well, it's because I had a baby a month ago." Gabrielle took a deep breath, but did not pause long, other than to see the shock on her mother's face. But before Elodie could ask any questions, Gabrielle held up her hand to her mother and kept talking. "That's why I went to stay with Corinne. She helped me through the whole experience, including the adoption agency that I used to put him up for adoption. Did I mention it was a boy? He was the sweetest thing I've ever seen on earth. They let me hold him for a moment before they took him. He was adopted on the same day I went home from the hospital." Gabrielle voice began to shake. "I'm so sorry I didn't tell you, I didn't know how or what to say, and once time passed to where it was several months, it was as though the window of opportunity closed. Then when Edgar told me about Corinne, and she invited me to stay with her and her aunt in Florida, everything kind of fell into place. I didn't want you to feel like you had to take any of this on yourself. I suppose, if I had kept the baby, it would have been different. He would even be with me here, now." Gabrielle sat there and waited for her mother to respond, and when she didn't, Gabrielle said, "I'm sorry, momma. I didn't mean to overwhelm you."

"You had a baby?" Elodie finally said. "And you gave him up for adoption? I thought you went to Germany for your education! What happened?"

"Momma, there are just some things I can't tell you right now. But I can assure you, that it was not my plan. Maybe someday this will make sense to me, too."

Elodie stood up and went into the kitchen where she poured herself a glass of ice water. "I need time to think about this. To let it sink in—how my own daughter could betray me like this. Months of being pregnant and the times we talked on the phone and you didn't tell me."

"It was never my intention to leave you in the dark about this. I wanted you to know. I just didn't know how to tell you," cried Gabrielle. "Mom, I know you're upset, but I have to go out right now. I have someone I need to see while I'm here and this might be my only chance. I will be back later tonight."

Elodie sat back down on the couch and looked up at her daughter. "You've changed. I knew Germany wasn't right for you."

"It's okay, mom. It's not Germany's fault just because it happened there." She picked up her purse and left, unable to face the disappointment on her mother's face anymore.

Once outside, Gabrielle took a deep breath. The second hardest part of her trip was over. But now, she was going to face the hardest part...finding and talking to Benji, and she knew just where to start.

I

"GABRIELLE?" SASHA OPENED her front door just moments after Gabrielle knocked on it. "My goodness, what are you doing here? I had no idea you were coming!"

The two girls hugged on the doorstep.

"I'm only here for a few days. I had to come see my mother, and of course you know I want to see Benji. Do you know where I can find him?"

"Yes, yes, of course. Come inside and have a glass of lemonade so we can catch up first. He is working and won't be off for another hour, so we have time. How have you been? The last I heard from you was your Christmas card."

"I know; it's been a rough year. But, I graduated school last spring, and get this! I have a sister!"

"You're kidding me. A sister?" Sasha poured two glasses of ice and lemonade, and directed Gabrielle to the living room couch. "Tell me!"

"Her name is Corinne. She lives in Florida, and she is Edgar's and my sister. She is amazing. I moved in with her in September." Gabrielle glanced up at the clock on the wall in hopes the next hour would fly by.

As much as she had missed Sasha, she really wanted to see Benji. She let Sasha talk for the most part, mostly because Gabrielle didn't want to tell her about the baby, and since that was what had absorbed her life for the past several months, she didn't have much else to say. So instead, she listened as Sasha told her about graduation and filled her in on the nuns and the other girls from school. Every few sentences Gabrielle glanced at the clock, only to see that the second hand had barely budged.

"I know! Let's go for a walk. Where did you say Benji is working?"

"He landed a job over at Capital Bank. It's a bit of a distance, so you may want to grab a taxi. I'll walk you to the taxi though."

"Okay," said Gabrielle as they both stood and went outdoors.

"He gets off work at four, so you should be there just in time," Sasha assured her.

As they walked, Gabrielle tried to keep the conversation light, but also on Benji. "So, he finished engineering school?"

"Yes. He's been at the bank for a little while now and has already moved up a few rungs on the ladder there. He's happy, Gabrielle. Here you go...a few taxis to choose from, even. Good luck, Gabrielle. Will I see you before you leave?"

"I'll try to stop by again. I'm only here for a few days, but will write to you from Florida if not." Gabrielle said, however she sensed she wouldn't see Sasha again during this trip.

As Gabrielle started walking toward the curb to hail a taxi, Sasha called to her one more time. "Oh, and Gabrielle, you should know that he is still with Roseline. But, I know he will be happy to see you."

Gabrielle felt a lump form in her throat, nearly sealing it closed. At least Sasha hadn't said the word marriage or married—she only said "with."

Gabrielle smiled at her friend, thanked her, and waved down the next taxi.

AS GABRIELLE SAT in the taxi, after giving the driver the address. She felt a sense of calmness come over her.

"This is your stop," the driver said.

As Gabrielle handed him a few bills, she looked up to see Benji leaving the bank and hailing his own taxi. Her heart pounded so hard she could hear it over the traffic and people passing by. She began to make steps closer to him, taking deep breaths with each one, and just as he hailed his own taxi, she softly called to him.

"Benji."

Benji looked around, until his eyes found her, and froze. He held a small briefcase in his left hand, and she was instantly reminded of how handsome he was. Gabrielle stood on the sidewalk, unable to take another step toward him. All that came between them were space and time. Every individual on the sidewalk—every vehicle on the road—every voice in the crowds—they all faded away. As though her feet had thawed her from her frozen state, Gabrielle began moving in his direction one step at a time. The ethereal silence broke when Benji spoke.

"Gabrielle? What on earth?"

Gabrielle took a final step toward him, and in unison they wrapped their arms around one another. Gabrielle never wanted to let him go.

Benji reached down and opened the door to the taxi he had just hailed. Gabrielle climbed in with Benji right behind her. He gave the driver an address that was just a block from their favorite tree. Intuitively he knew that was where they would go. They looked at each other nonstop as the taxi drove down the roads.

It wasn't until they climbed out of the taxi and walked the short distance down the path to their tree when Gabrielle spoke.

"I had to come see you." Her voice was shaking. "You never responded to my letters."

"Of course I did! I sent you several letters. Did you not get them?" The look of confusion on Benji's face immediately told Gabrielle that she had been right. Edgar had kept all of the letters. "I sent them to you at the address in Germany," he said.

"I never received them. Not one."

"To be honest, I stopped sending them by Christmas. None of your letters seem to indicate that you had received mine, which added to the confusion. Each of your letters told me you weren't getting mine, but I couldn't be sure. So, I stopped mailing any. I also stopped for another reason, though."

He looked down at the ground, kicking the dirt up with his foot. It was an action that Gabrielle immediately knew he was about to tell her what she didn't want to hear.

"Gabrielle, I'm with somebody. I've moved on." He held her hand, and found a way to look in her eyes when he told her the news.

"I know about Roseline. Sasha told me. But I needed to hear it from you, and even now that I have, I don't believe it's what you want. You know we belong together. It's always been that way." Gabrielle leaned in and rested her head on his shoulders. He wrapped his arms around her. "I should never have left," she whispered in his ear.

"Gabrielle, you know I love you. You know you will always be a part of me. But Roseline and I, well...we belong together. We've developed a bond while you were gone, and to tell you the truth, she needs me in ways you never did."

Gabrielle pulled back and looked right at Benji. "What? How could you say I never needed you?"

"I didn't say that. I said she needs me in certain ways that you didn't. My love, you proved that to me when you left. You left me for Germany," said Benji.

"All of your plans for your future were about you and your big dreams, none of them were about me or us."

"Are you kidding me? Everything was about us. Just because I left for some time doesn't mean we don't belong together. If anything, it strengthened my love for you by being away. I missed you so much. You have to know that from all the letters I sent." Gabrielle was shaking as her eyes pleaded with him.

"But, Gabrielle, Roseline is here with me every day. Our parents have met, the entire community knows we're dating. We have plans. Plans to get—" he stopped himself.

"Married? Are you marrying her?" Gabrielle's tone of voice suddenly changed, and took even her by surprise. The last thing she wanted to sound was desperate.

"Yes. We have plans to get married. I'm so sorry, Gabrielle. If I had known you were coming to visit..."

"What? What if you had known? Would you have told me not to come? Did you not want to see me? I'm sorry, but I needed answers. I never got your letters—"

A flash of Edgar reading then trashing her letters jumped in her mind and made her feel violated yet again.

"Yes, Sasha told me there was someone, but I had no idea what was going on, let alone that you were serious about marriage." Gabrielle nearly spat the last word out. "She only said there was talk of it. I don't know if knowing that would've changed whether or not I came, because you and I both know we belong together."

She stood tall and looked directly at Benji as she spoke, even though she wanted to crumble. His eyes drew her in the way they always had. She knew that if she hadn't seen him for fifty years, they would still do the same thing to her...make her melt.

"I don't know what else to say," said Benji. "I love you. I always will. I have all of your letters, and I keep them in a private place. I will always cherish them, and I'll always cherish you."

He leaned in and kissed her. It was not a goodbye kiss; it was one of their old kisses, the way they had always been, except this time, with her mouth pressed against his, it quivered for different reasons.

"Don't do this," she said while their lips were still touching. "Don't do it. Don't get married. Be with me. The last thing I said to you before I boarded that plane was that someday we would be together again. I meant that, Benji. I knew in my heart it would be true or I would not have written you nearly every day for the past year."

Those were the last words that she would speak that would ask Benji to choose her. She did not want to grovel or beg. She was too proud for that, but at the same time she knew what her heart felt.

"I simply can't be with you, Gabrielle," said Benji. "I don't expect you to understand, and I'm so very sorry for that. Look, I have to go now, and I honestly don't know what else to say. It was really wonderful to see you, and to get the answers we both needed, even if they are ones we don't agree upon. We are both now free to go on with our lives. I only ever wanted you to be happy, Gabrielle. I really did and still do. I want you to find someone who will give you all you deserve, who can support you in your dreams in ways I can't. My life is here in Haiti with my job and Roseline."

Gabrielle could no longer stand the pain his words were causing her. She kicked off her sandals, picked them up in her hands, and began running away—barefoot, and as fast as possible. Her sundress trailed in the wind, and even though the bottoms of her feet were hurting, she kept going. She did not stop until she reached home, where she slammed the front door and ran to her bedroom and slammed that door, too. Her childhood bed greeted her as she threw herself upon it for the last time.

AS THE PLANE lifted off the next day, Gabrielle looked out the window and down at Port-au-Prince. The place that had been home for the first seventeen years of her life sprawled out beneath the plane's wings. In time, as the altitude increased, it looked increasingly smaller and more distant. She thought about how in many ways she was too big to stay there. She knew she had much to do—a life to live that didn't involve staying there. As complicated as it was, it was also the truth she had known deep down and all along.

The only thing that Gabrielle could never wrap her head around was how she and Benji might have built a life together. There was no way he would ever leave Haiti, and there was no way she could ever return. She had trusted in God to show her how, but now as she sat in seat 7B of the aircraft, she wondered where the serenity was that God was meant to grant her. She wondered about the things she could not change. And now, she was forced to collect the courage within her in order to change the things she could—the parts of her life that she could control, like school. Most of all, however, she had to draw from her own wisdom. From that she would learn the difference between what she could change and what was left to the hand of God. These things, she knew, would be the first steps.

TURN THE PAGE FOR A SNEAK PEEK

AT THE NEXT

SERENITY DANCE SAGA

Serenity Dance: Un-Tango

FROM AUTHOR DANIELLE WAINWRIGHT

Chapter One

THE FLORAL PRINT curtain was so faded and tattered it nearly crumbled in her hands. She pushed it back so she could crack the window to let some air in. Even still, the thick humidity kept it from bringing much relief. They were too far inland to guarantee the ocean breeze would help. But, being early in the morning, at least the air would be on the cooler side for at least another hour.

Gabrielle pulled a cotton sundress on over her head. It was a red plaid that had faded to almost pink in the hot Florida sun. She then ran her fingers through her hair to tidy it up before leaving. With her book-filled backpack in hand, she slipped on her sandals and quietly closed the door as she left. She tried not to disturb her brother, Edgar, and his son, Emmanuel.

Business 203 was Gabrielle's first class at Florida International University that morning. Her professor was one who had zero tolerance for tardiness to his 8:30 AM class, but that was never an issue for Gabrielle. He was also a real stickler about not allowing food and drink into his classroom. He insisted that the noise caused by opening wrappers had caused him to go gray in previous years. He had put a stop to that five years ago. That meant that Gabrielle had to eat before class. Luckily, her walk to school wasn't very far, and she stopped at a gas station just a block away from school to grab a bottle of orange juice and a blueberry muffin. The wrapper around this muffin would have made her professor crazy because it was a thick plastic that she had to wrestle to open.

While inside the gas station, she ducked into the bathroom and splashed cold water on her face. Taking two sheets of paper towels, she blotted her face dry with one and dampened the other one, which she used to run up and down her arms to cool them off.

She arrived at school at 8 AM and sat on a brick wall outside the classroom to eat her breakfast. She pulled out her notes to review before class.

"Did you understand the homework?" The voice came from behind her. When Gabrielle turned and squinted into the rising sun, she smiled at the sight of her friend Monique.

"Yes, I finished it late last night. How about you? Any questions?" Even though the semester was barely underway, most of the students in her Business 203 class had pegged Gabrielle as the one to go to for help. It was an honor she was used to and relished in. In fact, it was one reason that she considered going into teaching.

"I think I got it, but can you just look at my answer to number five? That was the only one I wasn't too sure about." Monique sat down on the wall next to Gabrielle and handed over her notebook, which was already opened to the homework.

After a few moments of reading the page in front of her, Gabrielle said, "Yes, this is correct. You will do great in this class." Gabrielle handed the notebook back to Monique.

"Well, I don't know about great, but I do expect to at least pass." Monique squeezed her notebook back into her overstuffed backpack. "So, have you lived here long? In Miami, I mean?" she asked as she pulled out her own bottle of juice to finish before class. Hers was cranberry.

"No, not very long. I was staying with my sister until my brother and his son came over from Germany. I couldn't wait to start classes, though." When Gabrielle looked up, she happened to spot Edgar driving by. He was taking Emmanuel to elementary school, which was only a few miles down the road.

"Me, too. But, I'll be happier in three years, when we are up on the stage being handed our diplomas! That is, if I finish on time." Monique took the last sip of her cranberry juice and screwed the cap back on the bottle.

"Do you know what time it is?" asked Gabrielle.

"Yes," said Monique as she looked at her watch. "It's just eight twenty. Are you ready to go in?"

Gabrielle nodded, picked up her backpack, and on the way inside the building, tossed the bottle and wrapper into the garbage can.

She and Monique took two seats in the front row. They had buddied up on the first day of classes, and Monique had told Gabrielle that she didn't normally like having her back turned to the students behind her—it made her nervous—but she said it was worth it to sit next to Gabrielle. Even still, she looked over her shoulder at least ten times during class, something that Gabrielle found almost amusing if it weren't for the concerned look on Monique's face.

At the end of their first class, Gabrielle and Monique parted ways for different classes, but promised to meet in the library at five o'clock to do their homework. It was Gabrielle's second class that was a bit more entertaining; mostly due to Frederick, who sat behind her. He was the one who had an answer for all the professor's questions, but they always came with a comedic twist. Even though he was often correct with his answers, the jester's approach was beginning to wear on the professor. Since Frederick sat behind Gabrielle, attention was often targeted in their direction; something she had always welcomed in the past, but wasn't so sure now. She wondered if the professor would eventually stop calling on him.

The one thing she had noticed was that Frederick was always in his seat before she arrived. She could feel his eyes following her as she walked in and took her seat. She was partially flattered and partially disturbed by it, but either way she never made eye contact with him. The last thing she needed was for the professor to make a connection between the two. And she certainly wasn't looking to date anyone. Her focus was one hundred percent on school.

At five o'clock Gabrielle found Monique in the library where they compared notes for homework. They settled in to two chairs with large cushions and worked separately; however, Gabrielle was comforted by the companionship. She missed her friends, Sarah and Donna, from her high school in Germany. The threesome had been inseparable and when Gabrielle left Germany for Florida, she wondered if she'd ever find friends like them again. Having been a bit shy and always a terrific student, Gabrielle had always been one to make friends in school. However, they mostly wanted her help with homework and not much more. Sarah and Donna had been different. They taught Gabrielle the art of true friendship.

"Gabrielle, wake up..." Gabrielle woke up to Monique nudging her arm. "You fell asleep."

"Oh my goodness. What time is it?" Gabrielle asked..

"It's ten o'clock. The library is closing." Monique began shoving her books into her backpack and pulled Gabrielle's up off of the floor to hand to her. Once packed up, they left the library and started walking.

"Do you want me to walk you home?" asked Monique. "There are definitely streets you want to avoid this time of night. Trust me; I grew up here."

"Nice of you, but I'll be okay. It's not far."

"Okay, but don't let me read about you in the paper tomorrow," said Monique.

"Really, I'll be okay. The streets in Haiti weren't much better and I survived those. I appreciate the offer though."

"Haiti? You didn't tell me you were from Haiti."

"Yes, that's where I grew up before moving to Germany. I was only in Germany for a year—" Gabrielle exhaled, "and what a year it was. Maybe I'll tell you about it sometime. In the meantime, I'll see you tomorrow."

Gabrielle waved goodbye and turned the corner at the next block. The night air was still heavy with a pasty dew that stuck to her skin. Her sundress clung to her legs as she walked, making everything that much more uncomfortable. She was tired and her books were heavy. She fought to keep her eyes open as she walked down the next few blocks to her destination.

As she approached, she noticed a tiny light coming through the window, which meant Edgar was still up waiting for her. Emmanuel had most likely fallen asleep a few hours ago. He tired more readily in the heat of Miami than the colder and drier days in Germany.

He was adapting fairly well to his new school, all things considered, and seemed to be somewhat happy amongst the confusion of what his life had become in the past several months. All of their lives had turned upside down in a short amount of time, and they were just starting to get their footing back. For Emmanuel and Gabrielle, school was their escape.

Despite the late night heat, Gabrielle shivered as she approached the 1972 Dodge B-300 Xplorer van. She dreaded sleeping in it yet another night with her brother and his son just feet away with only an old black curtain between them. She pulled down on the handle and tried to open the door as quietly as possible so as not to waken Emmanuel.

"Where have you been?" Edgar hissed from behind the curtain. The smell of alcohol and stale body odor followed close behind his words.

"At the library with Monique. I fell asleep in the chair. It's been a long day. Goodnight."

Gabrielle slipped off her sundress and into the T-shirt she had worn for the past several nights straight. Edgar had promised they would go to the Laundromat as soon as he had the money. She pulled a cotton blanket over her and up to her chin. She couldn't sleep well without something over her. She fluffed her pillow, and by the time her head lay on it, she was already fast asleep.

CPSIA information can be obtained
at www.ICGtesting.com
Printed in the USA
FFOW03n2032241014
8345FF